"I've been thinking about the night of the shooting. My memory is like one of those old reel-to-reel films that's being restored. Sometimes the frames are out of order, but sometimes there are several frames intact together."

"You'd tried hypnotherapy when you first entered the witness protection program, right?" Luc asked.

"Yeah, but the doctor blamed me for not remembering. He said I was intentionally repressing the memories. I never went back to him."

"When did Mac mention it again?"

"When we were going over my initial witness statement to prepare for the trial. He asked if I would be willing to undergo hypnosis again. I agreed, as long as it wasn't with the previous doctor."

"Who else would know you were considering hypnosis again?"

"You don't think it's a coincidence that someone is trying to kill me now that I've resumed hypnotherapy?"

"No, I don't." Luc kept his voice low, his eyes never leaving her pale face. "I think someone doesn't want you to recall any more details about what happened that night."

Sarah Hamaker has written two nonfiction books, as well as stories for several *Chicken Soup for the Soul* books. She's a member of American Christian Fiction Writers and ACFW Virginia, as well as president of Capital Christian Writers Fellowship. She's also a parent coach with a weekly podcast called *You've Got This*. Sarah lives in Virginia with her husband, four children and three cats. Visit her online at sarahhamakerfiction.com.

Books by Sarah Hamaker

Love Inspired Suspense

Dangerous Christmas Memories

DANGEROUS CHRISTMAS MEMORIES

SARAH HAMAKER

HARLEQUIN® LOVE INSPIRED® SUSPENSE

Recycling programs
for this product may
not exist in your area.

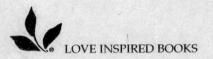

LOVE INSPIRED BOOKS

ISBN-13: 978-1-335-23248-9

Dangerous Christmas Memories

www.Harlequin.com

Printed in U.S.A.

This I recall to my mind, therefore have I hope.
It is of the Lord's mercies that we are not consumed,
because his compassions fail not. They are new
every morning: great is thy faithfulness.
—*Lamentations* 3:21-23

To my husband, Christian,
for his unfailing encouragement for my writing.

ONE

Priscilla Anderson set the blow-dryer on high and aimed the heat at Nancy's damp hair with one hand, a round brush in her other hand to smooth the slightly curly hair. Thank goodness the noise of the dryer meant Priscilla didn't have to pay attention to her client's incessant chatter. Today Nancy gushed about her recent trip to the Bahamas with her third husband over Thanksgiving. As she straightened Nancy's hair, Priscilla concentrated on keeping her hands steady enough that Nancy wouldn't notice she wasn't her usual self.

Priscilla clicked the dryer to a lower setting and began shaping the long bob to curl gently under Nancy's cheekbone. She sucked in a deep breath, letting it out slowly in an attempt to soothe her jitters as she sent up a silent prayer. *Lord, please keep me calm and safe from the man I think has been following me.*

Turning off the hair dryer, she was relieved to see Nancy had her attention on her phone. Good, no small talk necessary for a bit longer. After touching the surface of the curling iron quickly to judge its heat, Priscilla put the finishing touches on Nancy's hair.

"All done." Priscilla exchanged the curling iron for a handheld mirror, handing the latter to Nancy to view the haircut and style as she swiveled the chair around for her client to view her reflection.

The older woman admired her hair in the mirror. "Perfection like always. I told my yoga class to ask for you if they wanted a world-class haircut at a good price." Nancy smiled as Priscilla removed the salon cape with a snap. "You should move to one of those upscale places—your talents are hidden here."

Priscilla shook her head as she walked her client to the front of Snippy's, a chain of discount haircuts. "I appreciate your kind words, but this suits me just fine."

Nancy sighed. "You are too modest for your own good. But then again, I'm happy to pay only twenty-five dollars for an eighty-dollar haircut!"

Priscilla ran Nancy's credit card and handed her the slip to sign, glad that her hands had regained their steadiness. "Last time, you said you looked like a million bucks. I must be slipping."

The other woman laughed as she gave the receipt back to Priscilla with a generous tip scrawled on the bottom. "See you next month."

As Nancy exited the salon tucked into a strip mall, Priscilla caught a glimpse of a blond man in his late twenties—near her own age—lounging at one of the outdoor tables in front of the next-door coffee shop. She stepped closer to the floor-to-ceiling window, careful to keep her body partially hidden behind a decorated artificial Christmas tree positioned to the left of the front door. Unease coiled in her stomach like a strand of hair wrapping around a roller, tightening with a jerk as she recalled seeing the tall man behind her in a checkout line at the grocery store last night.

She had also seen him somewhere else before, but where? She closed her eyes briefly to pull up the memory. Ah, yes. Jogging by her apartment building Friday morning when she left for work. Now three days later, here he was again, outside her place of employment. Fairfax, Virginia, wasn't that big a city that she could attribute the sightings to mere coincidence.

Fishing her phone from her apron pocket, she surreptitiously snapped several photos of the man as he sipped from a cup while gazing down at his smartphone.

Heart pounding, Priscilla moved away from the window and through the salon toward the small break room next to the back door. With her next appointment in fifteen minutes, she had time to call Mac.

"Everything okay?" US Marshal James "Mac" MacIntire's voice had a sharp edge to it that Priscilla hadn't heard before. The married marshal had become like an older brother to her since becoming her point of contact three years ago.

"I think someone's following me." Priscilla paced the length of the empty room.

"Tell me more."

She relayed a description of the man. "The first time I noticed him, he was jogging by my apartment building. Last night, he was behind me in the checkout line at the grocery store. Now today he's outside the salon at the coffee shop next door. Perfectly legitimate actions but something tells me it's not accidental, that he meant to be in those places because I was there. I managed to take a couple of photos of him, but it was through a window, so it might not be clear. I texted them to you before I called."

"Let me pull them up."

Waiting while Mac accessed the photos, Priscilla concentrated on taking deep, controlled breaths to slow her racing heart. No sense in hyperventilating over what might be a coincidence. Her gut screamed that there was no way this guy just happened to show up exactly where she was at least three times in under a week.

"I emailed them to our tech guys to see what they can do to enhance them and trace his identity. He hasn't tried to approach you?"

"No." She kneaded the tight muscles in the back of her neck. "He's been kind of lurking in the background." She blew out a breath. "You know I don't see danger behind every bush. He's following me—that much I'm sure of."

"Do you think he's connected with our *friend*?" Mac voiced the very question that had occurred to Priscilla.

"If he is, I don't know why I'm still alive." She blinked back sudden tears at how comfortable she had been in her life here, that for a while, she'd managed to live like a normal person. If you called normal not being able to date or have close friends. If she stayed in witness protection much longer, she was afraid she'd never be comfortable getting close to anyone, given how superficial she had to keep all her relationships. With the very real potential of having to relocate at a moment's notice, she had grown used to her own company. But with the trial coming up, she'd begun to let herself think of what life could hold beyond witness protection, and that had heightened her sense of loneliness. "I can't believe I let my guard down enough to not notice someone was following me."

"Priscilla, don't beat yourself up. It happens to most people in the witness protection program." Mac's gentle tone soothed her. "We see it all the time in those who have been in WITSEC for more than a few years. And you've been in for seven."

She centered her thoughts back on the problem at hand, grateful for his reassurance. "What should I do?"

"For now, nothing. You know the best way to stay alive is to not panic, and any deviation from your normal routine could tip him off that you're onto him. Until we know what his agenda is, take extra precautions, have your go-bag ready and wait to hear from me. I'm headed into a briefing about our friend in five minutes, but then I'll come get you."

"Okay. I have clients scheduled through six today. I only hope I won't mess up their haircuts because of my nerves."

"I know I don't have to say this, but please, be careful." The seriousness of the way Mac delivered the platitude alerted Priscilla to just how shaken her handler was about the danger to her.

"I will." Priscilla said goodbye just as a bell tone on her phone's alarm rang to let her know she had a few minutes before her two o'clock appointment. She ducked into the single-stall restroom and locked the door. She needed to calm her inner turmoil or she'd never get through the rest of her shift.

Washing her hands, she gazed at her reflection in the mirror. It had been just over seven years since she witnessed the shootings that had thrown her into the US Federal Witness Protection Program. She had worked hard to change her appearance and her mannerisms. No longer did she bite her nails when nervous. Her formerly blond hair lay hidden underneath a rich brown hair coloring that she recently streaked with purple and turquoise. Her hair, which she used to keep short and spiky, now hung past her shoulders. Today she'd twisted it up into two side buns higher on the crown of her head than the typical "Princess Leia" hairstyle.

She looked nothing like the terrified cocktail waitress who'd hidden underneath a skirted serving cart in the kitchen of the Las Vegas Last Chance Hotel and Casino and seen through a slit in the fabric a man with a gun and silencer shoot three people in the head. The events of that night still had a hazy film on them, meaning that she had trouble recalling her exact movements or why she ended up hiding in the kitchen, but the memories of the shooting itself had been seared into her memory. The news that the hit man, Mason Culvert, had escaped custody while in the hospital after an emergency appendectomy had shaken her to the core. With Culvert's trial scheduled to begin just before Christmas, Priscilla feared the blond man could be connected to Culvert.

Leaving the bathroom, she walked toward the front of the store, passing three other stylists in various stages of cutting or styling their clients' hair. The blond man stood by the register, talking to the owner, Sandra Yu. Priscilla froze. Her pulse kicked into high gear. Before she could slip out the back door and contact Mac again, Sandra turned and spotted her.

"Priscilla?"

Priscilla considered ignoring the summons and bolting, but the blond man had had numerous opportunities to hurt her if he'd wanted to do so. That lessened her fear enough to allow her curiosity to pique as to why he had been following her—and what he was doing in the salon.

"Yes, Sandra?" Priscilla pasted a smile on her face and joined them.

"This is Mr. Long, your two o'clock." Sandra smiled at Mr. Long. "Priscilla's one of our best stylists."

"I've heard." His voice triggered a hidden awareness. She'd heard him speak before, but before the memory could resurface fully, the impression vanished.

Instead, Priscilla took a deep breath and gestured toward her station. "Right this way, Mr. Long." Cutting his hair would give her the perfect opportunity to question him under the guise of small talk—and wielding sharp scissors would offer some protection if his intentions weren't on the up-and-up. With another prayer for God's protection, she settled her client in the salon chair.

Lucas Benedict Langsdale III ran a hand through his shaggy hair. There had been a flicker of recognition in Priscilla's eyes when he spoke. Clearly, his voice had jarred a memory from their shared past, but other than that brief pause, she acted as if she didn't know him.

With effort, he kept his expression impassive. He'd play along with her game for a while, but soon enough he'd get the answers to questions he'd been waiting seven years to ask.

"Wash and cut?" Priscilla tapped the back of his chair.

"Both, please." At least that would buy Luc more time with her to see if she was pretending not to know him. A bride who skipped out on her husband mere hours after their wedding had a lot of explaining to do. Not that her explanation would make him change his mind about officially dissolving their short union.

She draped a cape around him, her fingers lightly skimming the back of his neck as she fastened the snaps. The large mirror directly in front of him afforded an opportunity to watch as she combed out his thick hair with gentle tugs.

Raising her eyes to meet his in the mirror, she cocked her head to one side. "You want the same style you currently have?"

"That sounds good. I like it a bit shorter around the

ears—can't stand to have hair in my ears." Luc closed his mouth, willing himself not to bombard her with questions about why she'd skipped out shortly after saying "I do." When he couldn't find her, Luc had filed a missing person's report with the Las Vegas police, which had turned up nothing. It was as if Priscilla had vanished into thin air. That first long year, he'd searched for her off and on, but eventually, he'd resigned himself to her not wanting to be found. Thinking that perhaps their Las Vegas wedding hadn't been legal after all, Luc had decided to forget the whole thing. But three years ago, an online post about a celebrity who had nearly committed bigamy because he had mistakenly thought his Las Vegas wedding license wasn't real pushed Luc to reinvestigate Priscilla's disappearance. After confirming through a Nevada attorney that their marriage was indeed legal, he had finally tracked her down.

"It's easier to cut your hair shorter first. Then I'll shampoo and style it." Priscilla picked up a pair of scissors, and Luc noticed her hand trembled slightly.

Maybe she wasn't as indifferent to his presence as he thought. Of all the scenarios he had imagined when coming face-to-face with Priscilla again, Luc had never anticipated a total lack of recognition. *God, what should I do now—ask my questions or wait to see what she says?*

He stayed silent as her fingers in his hair brought forward vivid memories of their time together at the Last Chance Hotel and Casino in Las Vegas. He closed his eyes, letting go for a moment all the unanswered questions, and tried to relax as she touched his hair.

The front window shattered and an object zipped by him. His eyes popped open as someone screamed. Then something whizzed by his chest, striking the wall to the right of him with a thump.

"That's gunfire!" Luc slid out of the chair onto the floor as the *pop-pop-pop* of three consecutive shots mingled with the sound of more breaking glass. Shards from the mirror at Priscilla's station rained down on his head. Where was Priscilla?

Luc shook his head to rid it of bits of glass as he frog-walked behind the next station, then saw Priscilla running toward the back of the store. *Lord, please keep her safe. Help me to protect her.* Another hail of bullets shattered more glass and mirrors, eliciting another round of screams from stylists and clients hiding behind stations and chairs. Sirens wailed in the distance but there wasn't time to wait for law enforcement to rescue Priscilla.

He used two vanities as cover, but had to take the last few feet in the open. As he bent over and headed down the short hallway where he'd seen Priscilla go, something buzzed past his left upper arm, bringing with it a short burst of pain. Ignoring it, Luc pressed forward just in time to see Priscilla fling open a door marked Private.

Luc reached the opened door seconds after her and hurled himself inside. His heart pounded as he straightened and spotted the back exit door just closing. Catching the door before it closed, he burst through it into a narrow alleyway behind the strip mall with a large stand of trees opposite.

A quick look to the left showed nothing, but to the right, Priscilla had nearly reached the end of the alleyway. The sound of gunfire faded as sirens indicated first responders had reached the shopping center. Behind the strip mall, the stillness belied the chaos that had erupted on the other side of the buildings. Luc shook off the throbbing of his left arm and ran after her, catching up as she veered through the trees on a dirt path he hadn't seen from the alleyway. Just inside the woods, she paused near a junction where the dirt trail connected with a wider paved one, panting with her hand on her side.

"Are you okay?" He struggled to control his own breathing, which came out in gasps.

She nodded. "Just winded."

"Thank God." Luc couldn't quite process what had happened. "Someone was shooting into the salon." He gently shook his head to dislodge more pieces of glass. Why would someone fire a gun into a hair salon on a slow Monday afternoon?

Priscilla pulled out her cell phone and punched in a number. "Shots fired. At the salon. Person we discussed earlier with me. We're on the trail behind the shopping center."

Luc almost didn't catch her wording. A person she'd discussed earlier with who? He would have to figure out what she meant later, when he wasn't winded from running from an active shooter. His left arm pulsated with pain as the adrenaline started to ebb.

For now, he kept his attention on Priscilla. Her breath hitched as she held the phone to her ear with a hand that shook.

Then a couple with two puppies straining at their leashes rounded the corner. Luc immediately moved to shield Priscilla from the strangers.

One of the puppies stopped to sniff Luc's shoe. The man laughed as he tugged on the leash. "Sorry, he's the overly friendly one."

From the couple's calm demeanor, they must not have heard the shots as they approached the shopping center from the rear path. Luc wasn't about to enlighten them and murmured, "That's okay," as the man attempted to move the dog away from Luc.

The woman gasped as the puppy's nose came up from the ground red. "You're bleeding!"

Luc glanced at his upper arm. Blood he hadn't noticed until now dripped down his sleeve and splashed onto the ground by his foot. He clamped his right hand over the wound. Sudden light-headedness washed over him, and he concentrated on breathing evenly to avoid passing out.

"Honey, call 911. That's an awful lot of blood," the woman said to her companion, who immediately whipped out his phone and punched in the numbers.

Luc started to agree, but one look at Priscilla's face told him that she was not going to wait for an ambulance. She had already started to edge away to the right from the couple on the path, her voice low as she continued her conversation on the phone.

Although his arm ached and probably needed medical attention, Luc didn't want to let her out of his sight *again*. Why hadn't Priscilla panicked when the bullets started flying?

Now he had more questions that needed answers.

TWO

Priscilla had to tamp down her fear if she was to get out of this situation alive. She paced a few steps away from the couple and Mr. Long to talk quietly with Mac on her phone, her nerves jangling. She concentrated on slowing down her inhalation and exhalation.

"Was anyone hurt?" Mac snapped out the question. He had moved into crisis mode and she wasn't about to let his briskness hurt her feelings.

"Yes, a bullet hit the upper left arm of Mr. Long. I don't think it's bleeding too bad. I don't know if anyone was hit in the salon because I got out of there as fast as I could." She sneaked a glance at Mr. Long, who had his right hand clamped on the wound.

"We need to get you out of there pronto. Your safety is top priority." Mac's reminder of the danger that still permeated the very air around her didn't settle her nerves.

"Unfortunately," Mac continued, "it could take me about thirty minutes to get to Fairfax. You can't wait where you are. Still too close to the salon for my peace of mind."

"My car's in the parking lot near the salon." Priscilla breathed in and out to the count of ten. Her brain kicked back into gear. "I only have my wallet." She voiced her thoughts as she took in her surroundings. "And I have my phone. There's a bus stop farther along this path. Hold on a minute." She consulted the Next Bus app on her phone, then clicked back to Mac. "The Gold 1 Cue bus is due to arrive in less than ten minutes. Why don't you text me where to get off once I board at the Daniels Run/Lee Highway stop?"

"Yes, got it."

"See you soon." She disconnected the call and eased a look over her shoulder. The woman handed her leash to her companion and drew out a bandanna from her back pocket to wrap around Mr. Long's arm. It was time for Priscilla to move.

Priscilla stepped away without the group noticing. She didn't want to abandon the man who had been shot on her account, but she also didn't want to endanger him further, which she would if she stayed with him. The man who was after her would have no bones about shooting her and whoever she was with—of that she had no doubt. Priscilla took a bigger step and crunched a dry twig with her shoe.

"Hey, don't leave!" Mr. Long extracted himself amid the woman's protest that they had called for an ambulance.

"You should stay here, get help for your arm," Priscilla said, then broke into a run down the path. Too much time had been wasted already. The shooter could be around the back of the building searching for her. He'd find the path easily enough. She had to be on the bus heading to Mac and safety.

A branch snapped behind her. She risked a glance to see Mr. Long, his face pale, jogging along the trail. He should be waiting for medical attention, not following her.

Ignoring him, she slowed slightly to check the Next Bus app. The Gold 1 Cue bus would arrive in seven minutes at the closest stop. The next bus heading in the right direction wouldn't be coming for another thirty minutes—she definitely couldn't wait around for that one.

Priscilla increased her pace, pushing through the stitch in her side. If only she liked running, she'd be in better shape. Her lungs burned as she sucked in more air before checking the time on the app again. Four minutes to the bus's arrival. Right up ahead, Priscilla saw the trail spur to the street on the left and took it, pulling on her reserves to make it up the steeper incline without slowing her speed.

Mr. Long grunted as he tried to keep up. Her conscience chided her for caring only for her own skin and not about whether he would pass out on the trail. But he didn't have to follow her.

"You should have waited for medical help," she said over her shoulder.

The man merely shook his head, and she turned her attention back to the path. Somehow, as she cut his hair, she hadn't been afraid of him. After living for years fearful of her fellow human beings, she had learned to trust her instincts when it came to who she could trust and who she couldn't. The way he'd thanked God for her safety and stepped between her and the dog walkers had reaffirmed what her gut had told her—that she could trust him. Too bad, she would have to find a way to lose him before his association with her got him killed.

Priscilla reached the edge of the woods and halted to check the bus arrival time once more. Craning her neck to view the street, she saw that everything appeared normal. A woman with a baby in a stroller and a preschooler holding on to the handle waited at the bus stop. That meant Priscilla could hang back at the tree line until the bus approached the stop.

"Why were you running? Shouldn't we have waited to talk with the police?" Mr. Long braced himself against a tree, his complexion gray.

"You need to see a doctor." Priscilla feared Mr. Long would collapse right there. If he did, she would miss her bus, because she couldn't just leave a hurt man to fend for himself, not when he was injured on her account.

"I *need* to speak with you."

The simplicity of his request startled her, and an alarm bell rang inside her head. She narrowed her eyes. "You *are* following me."

Mr. Long stayed bent over, his forehead resting against his right arm propped on the tree. "You noticed?"

Priscilla ticked off the incidents on her fingers. "The grocery store, jogging by my apartment building, today outside Snippy's. Here beside me now. You weren't exactly subtle."

The man shifted upright with a wince. Then his eyes closed and his body slumped toward the tree.

"Oh, no, you don't." Priscilla hastened to his side and grabbed his right arm. "Don't you faint on me." She slung the arm over her shoulders, nestling underneath to support him. "You need to stay upright."

"I'll be okay," he mumbled against her hair. "Just give me…a minute."

Priscilla didn't have a minute. The bus rumbled up to the curb. Taking him with her presented its own set of problems, but she had no time to dither over a decision. Better take him with her—at the very least, she could find out why he had been following her.

"I don't have a minute. The bus is here, and I need to get on it." Without another word, she started off toward the bus. To her relief, he stayed upright and leaned on her only a little bit.

"Bus? But my car's in the parking lot." His words came out a bit slurred as if pain was dulling his senses.

"No time. Now keep quiet." Priscilla dug a ten-dollar bill out of her work apron and fed it into the meter. "For both of us," she told the driver, an older woman wearing a Santa hat with cropped hair and a name tag that read Charlene Grant.

Charlene eyed Mr. Long with an apprehensive expression. "What happened to him?" the driver asked as Priscilla gathered her change from the machine.

"You know how men are." She gave Charlene a rueful smile. "A teensy cut and he goes all woozy on me." She jerked her head toward the bandanna. "He'll be all right."

Charlene chuckled. "If you say so."

Priscilla hustled Mr. Long to the back of the bus, plopping him down in the corner, then sitting down beside him as the bus pulled away from the curb.

With deft movements, she untied her work apron with the word *Snippy's* and a logo of an animated pair of smiling scissors. At least she had some cash, thanks to the generous tips of her customers. Stuffing the bills into her wallet, she checked to make sure the driver's attention wasn't on her and Mr. Long, then shoved the apron underneath her seat. No sense advertising where she worked, especially once the news broke about the shooting.

"You want to tell me what's going on?"

Priscilla whipped her head to stare into Mr. Long's deep blue eyes tinged with pain. "Why are you following me?"

A ghost of a smile crossed his lips. "You always answer a question with a question?"

"When I haven't gotten an answer the first time I asked it, yes." Something about him triggered a feeling that she should know him. Their encounter hadn't been recent—of that she was sure. Which meant it predated the shooting that thrust her into witness protection and running for her life. But she'd had so few friends back then and none of them had been a hunky, tall blond man.

"Why am I following you?" The man drew in a steadying breath and let it out slowly. A little color returned to his cheeks. "Because I couldn't believe I'd finally found you after years of searching."

A frisson of fear sliced into her. "You've been looking for me for years?" She stiffened her spine. It was too late to double guess her decision now. She was stuck with the man.

"Yes, for a very long time." He held her gaze, his eyes both demanding and pleading with her for what, she didn't know. All she knew was that she couldn't look away.

Her phone pinged, indicating an incoming text. She tore her gaze away to check, glad for an excuse to break eye contact. Mac's text was brief: Traffic better than expected. Get off at the stop by Chick-fil-A. Waiting there.

The bus eased into Fairfax Circle from Old Lee Highway, then swung onto Fairfax Boulevard. The stop Mac indicated would be the next one. She pulled the signal string. "This is our stop." She would let Mac finish questioning why Mr. Long had been searching for her.

Luc gritted his teeth against the discomfort in his arm. The bullet had gone straight through the upper flesh of his arm, which still seeped some blood through the bandanna. So much for behaving like a man in front of Priscilla. She'd had to practically carry him onto the bus. At least she hadn't left him in the woods, where he had almost passed out. Why she took him with her he didn't know, especially as it had become obvious to him that she had no clue who he was. No one could fake that look of unrecognition. The pain of her not recognizing him cut deeper than the bullet.

The bus ground to a halt, and Priscilla rose. "Do you need any help?"

He shook his head as he struggled to stand while a wave of dizziness crashed over him. By sheer willpower, he managed to exit the bus without falling flat on his face. *Thank You, Lord.*

Once off the bus, Priscilla paused as the driver re-entered traffic after picking up passengers. She pointed to a black SUV idling by the curb. "That's our ride."

Luc nodded and followed behind her at a slower pace. He placed his hand on the side of the car to steady himself, pleased he hadn't stumbled and fallen to the ground during the short walk. Priscilla reached the vehicle first and spoke to the driver through the open window.

Priscilla opened the back door. "Get in."

Probably not a good idea to climb into a car driven by a stranger, but the truth was, he didn't think he could stand on his own two feet much longer. Besides, he didn't want to lose sight of Priscilla again. In he climbed, with Priscilla right behind him. The dark interior warmed his body, the back windows heavily tinted. A man in the front had short-cropped hair and wore dark shades and a Bluetooth headset in his ear.

"Did anyone else follow you?" the man asked Priscilla in clipped tones, smoothly merging the SUV into the late-afternoon traffic on Fairfax Boulevard.

"I don't think so, but I can't be sure."

"Right." The man threw a glance at Luc in the mirror. "How's your arm?"

Luc glanced down at the bandanna covering the wound. The gray bandanna with pink Yorkshire dogs had only a bit of red smudged along one edge. "Okay. I think it's stopped bleeding."

"We'll get it checked out when we arrive." The man turned his attention back to the road, his eyes moving from the rearview mirror, to the side mirrors, to the windshield.

"Where are we going?" Luc should have asked that question before getting into the SUV, but where Priscilla was going, he was along for the ride.

"That's on a need-to-know basis," the man stated calmly. "Priscilla, you'll find a first-aid kit under the front passenger seat."

Luc closed his eyes as the SUV continued north on Fairfax Boulevard. He wanted to ask who the driver was, question why he couldn't be told their destination, why Priscilla had called this man after the shooting, and a million more questions. But a wet blanket of tiredness and pain settled over him, dulling his senses.

"Mr. Long?" Priscilla's voice brought him back to reality.

He opened his eyes, focusing on her warm brown ones. Wait a minute. Priscilla had had blue eyes—not a bright vivid blue like his own, but a softer shade like the sky after a gentle summer rain. No, he was sure this was the woman he had married. He wanted to ask her why she acted like she didn't know him, but with his brain fuzzy from the pain, he should wait until his head was clear to tackle such questions.

"Here's some ibuprofen for your pain. I'm sorry we don't have something to wash them down with." Priscilla ripped open a single-dose pill packet.

When he extended his right hand, she shook the pills into it.

Luc tossed the ibuprofen in his mouth and dry swallowed. "Thanks." He closed his eyes again, but couldn't help asking one of his many questions. "You were going to leave me in the woods. Why didn't you?"

She sighed. "Because I'm responsible for your getting shot."

THREE

Luc's eyes popped open. "How could you have known someone would start shooting into the hair salon?"

Priscilla didn't answer, but exchanged a look with the driver. Something wasn't right here. Even his pain-dulled brain picked up on the undercurrent of concern—no, fear—that hummed around Priscilla. Why would she still be afraid when they'd escaped the shooter?

He hadn't realized he'd voiced that last question aloud until the driver responded. "I'm asking the questions. Who are you? Why were you following Priscilla?"

Luc frowned. Priscilla had asked the same thing, but he hadn't had time to answer her fully. He wasn't sure he wanted to blurt out the entire story in front of a man with whom Priscilla was acquainted but of whom he knew nothing. "I could ask you the same question— who are you?"

The man executed a sharp right turn onto a business street that ran parallel with the main road. "I'm US Marshal James MacIntire."

A US marshal? Luc blinked. He might have guessed law enforcement from the way MacIntire carried himself, but he wouldn't have pegged him as a marshal. "I thought marshals hunted fugitives."

"They do." MacIntire cut his eyes to the rearview mirror, then the two side mirrors. He punched something on the middle console that Luc couldn't see from his vantage point behind the passenger's seat. "We've got company. A silver Ford Explorer with North Carolina plates Charlie, zebra, delta, one, three, five." He repeated the plate number, listened for a moment, then disconnected the call.

"I was followed?" Priscilla sounded scared and angry at the same time. "I'm sorry, Mac."

Mac. The person she'd been talking to on the trail. Then he remembered the other job marshals had—witness protection.

As Mac whipped the car into the parking lot of an apartment complex and exited on the back end into a residential neighborhood, Luc turned to Priscilla, who gripped the grab bar with one hand while the other remained fisted on her lap. Her fear, the certainty with which she knew the shooting at the salon had been because of her, Priscilla's reluctance to share anything with him, and her observation of his presence on the fringes of her life instantly made perfect sense to him. She was in the US Federal Witness Protection Program.

That knowledge didn't alleviate his concern that she didn't recognize him. Luc would puzzle that out later, but he could clarify what was happening right now. That knowledge brought a fierce need to protect her from whatever danger she was in, despite the fact that she had deserted him directly after marrying him. As Mac executed an illegal rolling stop at a deserted intersection, Luc quietly said to Priscilla, "You're in witness protection, aren't you?"

Priscilla gaped at Luc. "What did you say?"

Luc patiently repeated the question, relieved that the

ibuprofen had indeed dulled the pain and given him back some of his mind.

Her expression shuttered, giving him no clue as to her thoughts. "Who are you, Mr. Long?"

Luc gave her a pass on not answering his question. Maybe hearing his name would jingle a bell in her memory. "For starters, my name isn't Mr. Long. It's Lucas Benedict Langsdale the third." Saying his full name always sounded pompous to his ears. Blast his father for naming him after his paternal grandfather, who had been named for an ancestor who had died in the mid-1800s.

She raised her eyebrows, a slight smile playing across her lips. "The third, hmm? The second must be your father, then?"

"The second is my grandfather, still alive and kicking at the ripe old age of eighty-five. I go by Luc, while my grandfather's Lucas." He neatly steered the conversation back to Priscilla. "But my name is not important. Why are you hiding out in witness protection?"

Mac turned right onto Annandale Road as a newscaster on the radio read the top-of-the-hour news at 3:00 p.m. "Priscilla isn't at liberty to discuss the matter."

"Let me guess—that information is on a need-to-know basis, and I don't need to know." Luc would have to be content with having his suspicions nearly one hundred percent confirmed.

Mac frowned, his head swiveling to look over his left shoulder.

"What's wrong?" Priscilla craned her neck to look in the same direction.

Luc started to look as well, but the movement jostled his arm, so he stayed put.

"I thought a truck was getting too close, but it eased

back." Mac shifted in his seat and directed his attention to the traffic in front of him.

Priscilla resettled in her seat, but kept her hand braced against the door. "Is it the Explorer again?"

"No, a beat-up Toyota pickup without a front license plate." Mac made a right turn onto Arlington Boulevard, then accelerated into the left lane of the divided four-lane highway.

Priscilla gulped beside him as the vehicle wove in and out of traffic. "What's happening?"

As they approached the Wilson Boulevard intersection, Mac whipped the SUV into the right-hand lane as the traffic light at the intersection flicked from green to yellow. Luc leaned slightly to see the view in the driver's-side mirror. A dirt-caked truck mimicked their SUV's every move, staying right on their bumper.

Luc shifted to see out the windshield as the traffic light turned red, sending up a prayer for safety as Mac hit the gas. Then the truck slammed into the rear of the car, sending it spinning into oncoming traffic.

Priscilla screamed as Mac wrenched the wheel to miss a collision with a minivan hurtling toward them from the right. Their SUV skidded as Mac fought to bring the vehicle under control.

"Watch out! He's coming again!" Mac maneuvered the car onto Wilson Boulevard, a one-way thoroughfare, just as the SUV shook with another hit from behind. Metal screeched as the other vehicle seemed to push the SUV along. Mac struggled to keep the SUV moving forward in the left lane. A shopping center parking lot entrance loomed on the left, and Mac swerved into it.

Hands shaking, Priscilla looked behind her in time to take a mental snapshot of the battered pickup zooming away, its license plate smeared with mud. Mac eased the SUV into the parking lot of an Asian supermarket, picking a spot away from other cars.

"Everyone okay?" Mac put the SUV into Park.

"I'm all right." Priscilla looked at Luc, who offered a tiny shrug. "Mr. Langsdale's hanging in as well."

"Good. We'd better get moving again." Mac put his hand on the ignition as sirens wailed closer. "Looks like someone called the cops."

Priscilla twisted around to see two police cruisers pull into the parking lot and head toward their SUV. Her stomach flip-flopped. Mac had told her that local law enforcement wasn't always cooperative with marshals and their witnesses. She didn't want to wait for the officers to question them and fill out paperwork—she wanted to get as far away from Fairfax, Virginia, as she could to a safer location.

The cruisers parked behind them. Mac disconnected his phone from the console and dialed a number, telling whoever answered, "We're in a spot of trouble." He detailed the incident, describing the truck and their location with precision.

Luc nudged her shoulder.

Priscilla jerked her head toward him, her hands wrapped tightly together.

"Are you okay?" He nodded toward her jiggling knee. "You seem very agitated. Surely that truck driver is long gone, and we have two police cruisers parked right behind us."

How could she explain that none of that mattered, not if the person who was after her decided today was the day he would finally end her life? She stilled her leg. "You don't understand. We need to get out of here, not stay like sitting ducks."

Mac put down his phone. "The officer is coming up to the car. Let me do the talking." Without waiting for confirmation from Luc or Priscilla, he powered down the driver's-side window, then kept his hands visible on the steering wheel as a tall black policeman paused a foot from the car. Mac pasted a smile on his lips. "Officer, I'm a US marshal and I'm carrying a weapon. May I reach into my left breast pocket to show you my ID?"

"Please keep your hands where I can see them." The officer peered over Mac's shoulder into the interior, his eyes spotting Priscilla and Luc. With his hand on his gun at his right hip, the cop spoke something into his shoulder mic. Then the officer addressed Mac. "Who else is in this vehicle?"

Mac pushed his sunglasses up on the top of his head with his left hand, then placed it on the top of the door in full view of the cop. "Officer, there are two passengers in the back seat."

The policeman moved a step back from the SUV. "Sir, I'm going to need you and your passengers to exit the vehicle."

Another police officer had left his cruiser to stand a few feet from the passenger's side of the SUV hood. As the air filled with tension, Priscilla's heart began to pound. The taut stance of the cops radiated suspicion, but she couldn't get out of the SUV without exposing herself to a potential assassin who might be lurking nearby. She didn't want to find out if the shooter had improved his or her aim.

She focused her attention on Mac, who appeared unruffled, relaxed even, by the officer's request.

Mac smiled. "I would be delighted to get out, but I'm afraid my passengers will have to stay put." He kept his voice pleasant yet firm. "As I mentioned, I'm a

US marshal. Someone with professional driving skills deliberately rammed into our vehicle, pushing us into oncoming traffic."

The officer considered his words for a long moment. "Let me see your credentials."

"Of course, Officer. I'm going to reach into my left breast pocket with my right hand." Mac put actions to his words, moving slowly to extract his badge folder.

The cop accepted the leather folder and flipped it open, his eyes moving from the creds to Mac's face and back again. "I'll be right back."

The second officer stayed in position, his hand on the gun butt, while the other cop walked back to his cruiser.

"What happens now?" Priscilla didn't want to sit here a moment longer than absolutely necessary.

"We wait while he calls it in." Mac's phone rang, and he tapped the screen to activate the hands-free app. "Mac here." A short pause, then Mac succinctly brought the caller up to speed on their present situation.

Priscilla fidgeted in her seat, wanting to be doing something, anything, other than hanging tight. Eavesdropping on Mac's call distracted her from her fear that the person after her might suddenly appear and start shooting again.

"As soon as we're finished here, we'll go to location five, zero, alpha, Charlie, eight," Mac told the caller.

She twisted in her seat to see what the police officers were doing. The cop who had approached their vehicle got out of the police cruiser and headed back toward the SUV.

"Okay, will do." Mac ended the call. "How are you doing, Mr. Langsdale?"

"Hanging in there." Luc, with his eyes closed and his head leaning against the seat back, spoke in a voice that sounded thready. "That last maneuver slammed my hurt arm against the door."

"Hopefully, we'll be on our way soon and get that wound looked at." Mac tapped his fingers against the steering wheel. "But it would delay us if Fairfax County's finest saw a wounded man in my back seat."

"I understand." Luc winced.

"He's coming back to the car. Stay quiet." Mac replaced his hands on the steering wheel, his posture laid-back.

Priscilla held her breath as she saw in the driver's-side mirror the approach of the officer, Mac's badge folder in his hand.

"Here you go, Marshal." The officer handed Mac his ID through the open window.

Fear gripped Priscilla hard as her stomach clenched. *Please, let us go.*

"It'll be okay," Luc reassured her in a quiet voice. "Remember, God is the one in control."

She looked at Luc, whose steady gaze held a calmness she didn't feel. He didn't know it would be okay, but the reminder of God's sovereignty and Luc's composed expression relaxed her agitation.

The second officer suddenly moved back to his cruiser. Then he straightened to call to the officer still by Mac's open window. "We've got a 401 in progress at the convenience store on Patrick Henry Drive."

"Right behind you." The cop turned back to Mac. "We're finished here." The officer walked back to his police cruiser and climbed in before turning on the siren and roaring away down Wilson Boulevard.

Mac started the SUV, then pulled onto the street. "We're going to go to a safe house. It's too dangerous to go back to your apartment. Someone will pack up your things later. Anything you can't live without at the apartment?"

Priscilla thought about the sparsely furnished one-bedroom she'd called home for the past five years. While she had accumulated the usual detritus of life—books, DVDs, a few keepsakes from day-trip excursions around the area—there was nothing personal about those things, nothing that couldn't be easily replaced. "No."

Mac must have heard the sadness in that one syllable. "This will be over soon. We will catch the person responsible for this and you will get your life back."

"I know." Priscilla didn't know what else to say. Mac was doing his job to keep her safe, and in turn she would do hers by obeying his instructions to the letter. The best way to stay alive was to do what the marshals said—she had had that drilled into her during the transition period. With Culvert on the loose again, she wasn't about to jeopardize her own safety by doing something stupid like branching out on her own.

Priscilla closed her eyes as the last bit of adrenaline seeped out of her body and in its place a blanket of tiredness took up residence. As the SUV sped toward safety, she couldn't help but wonder if she had been living an illusion of security that had come crashing down.

FOUR

Luc jolted awake when the SUV stopped. He couldn't believe he had fallen asleep. The combination of the shooting, car accident and ibuprofen must have lulled him into catching a few winks. Stretching his back sent a stabbing pain in his arm, which receded to throbbing. Careful not to move his injured limb, he pulled out his phone to check the time. 6:38 p.m. They had been driving for around three hours.

Mac shifted in the driver's seat to face the back and spotted Luc's phone. "You'll need to give me your phone, Mr. Langsdale."

"My phone?" Luc wasn't about to hand over his smartphone without an explanation. "Why do you need it?"

"Because you're now in witness protection along with Priscilla. For security, you can't contact anyone until we apprehend the man who's after her. I'd have asked for it earlier, but you were sleeping."

Luc shook the last of the cobwebs from his brain, his hand clutching the phone in a tighter grip. "What if I don't want to go into witness protection? I have a choice, right?"

Mac exchanged a look with Priscilla, who stayed silent. "To enter the program permanently, you would have to agree to do so. However, this would be temporary. My top priority is keeping Priscilla safe, and right now, you're along for the ride."

"What does that mean?" Luc still kept his phone, not willing to hand over the device so easily.

"That you'll need to stay in the safe house with Priscilla for a day or two while we get this sorted out," Mac replied. "We'll have marshals on guard around the clock while we figure out where to permanently relocate her. With your being a witness to the salon shooting, you might have noticed something that can help us catch whoever's behind this."

Luc had a hard time digesting that information. But the idea that he'd be able to talk more with Priscilla appealed to him. "Will I be able to at least let my family and employer know I'll be gone for a couple of days?"

Mac shook his head. "Tell me who to text or email and what to say, and I'll send it for you."

Luc studied the marshal's granite jawline. The other man wasn't going to budge. Luc reluctantly reached over the seat to give Mac the phone. "I'm glad you take keeping Priscilla safe seriously, but I have to ask—do you trust anyone?"

"I wish I could trust people, but unfortunately, most of them think precautions like not using their smartphone for anything don't apply to them." Mac's face settled into grim lines. "Witnesses can die because someone didn't follow these rules. Now, who needs to know you'll be taking a few days off?"

Luc gave Mac the name of his boss and a message about a family emergency that necessitated his immediate absence from his job with CS Enterprises, a cybersecurity company with government contracts. He also gave Mac a message to give his sister, with whom he was expected for dinner the next evening. He used a sudden trip to work for a client who insisted on no outside phones while working on the company's highly sensitive computer network.

Priscilla raised her eyebrows. "Wow, those are really good excuses. Sounds like you've had practice in covering your real whereabouts."

"Not at all. Just read too many spy thrillers, I guess." He shrugged. "I just hope those excuses work. I'd hate for anyone to be worried about me or think I'm missing."

Mac powered off Luc's phone and pocketed it. "I'll make sure you get it back."

"Are we waiting for backup?" Priscilla's left leg started jiggling again. She looked up to see Luc watching her leg and stopped the movement.

"Yes, should be here soon." Mac continued to survey their surroundings.

Luc gazed at the small house tucked into a side street of what appeared to be a quiet neighborhood. Many of the houses had Christmas lights, the bright displays a welcome sight after their harrowing trip. The mild early-December day hadn't brought anyone outside, although most driveways had cars parked in them.

Another vehicle pulled parallel with theirs in the gravel driveway and four clean-shaven men in nearly identical suits stepped out. Reinforcements had arrived. Two of the men fanned out to check the house perimeter, while the other pair disappeared inside. After a few minutes, one of the men who had entered the house gave a hand signal to Mac from the front stoop.

"Mac? Can we get out of the car?" Priscilla sounded tired and scared.

"Yes, let's go into the house." Mac exited the SUV,

giving the area a sweep before opening Priscilla's door. As she got out, Luc opened his own door and eased to a standing position. His whole body ached even though it was his upper arm that had been creased by a bullet.

He followed the pair into the small Cape Cod–style house with two dormer windows. The avocado-green shag carpet in the living room affirmed the home hadn't been updated since it was built in the early seventies. A small kitchen with the same color appliances sat to the right and a short hallway led to what Mac said was a bedroom and adjoining bathroom.

One of the two men who had cleared the house stood in the kitchen doorway. "Mr. Langsdale? If you'll come through to the kitchen, I'd like to take a closer look at your arm."

Luc wasn't surprised they knew his identity. Mac had likely relayed that information soon after Luc had told Priscilla his real name. What he didn't know was how deep into his background the marshals would look at first glance. Luc needed to talk with Priscilla first about their wedding, but that would have to wait until he'd had something to eat and some rest. His brain in its current state was too muddled to think straight.

He followed the man into the kitchen, where the second marshal had laid out first-aid supplies—gauze, bandages and a syringe.

"What's that?" Luc pointed to the syringe.

"Antibiotics." The man grinned. "Don't worry—I'm a trained paramedic as well as a US marshal." He held out his hand to Luc. "By the way, I'm Nick Grayson. Have a seat and let me see that arm."

Luc shook his hand, then joined Grayson at the table. From the open doorway, he could see Priscilla and Mac conferring in the living room, standing close together.

Mac, with his wavy brown hair and muscular form, appeared like a TV version of a US marshal. Luc didn't spot a wedding ring on Mac's hand. Maybe Priscilla was in love with her handler, which would make asking her for an annulment that much easier.

"Stay still while I remove the bandage." Grayson nodded toward the other room. "Don't worry. Mac's married."

Embarrassment crept over Luc like an old man shoving on a baseball cap. "I don't know what you're talking about."

"Sure you don't." Grayson swiped the area around the wound with an alcohol swab, then used a saline rinse to cleanse the wound itself. "Not that I blame you. She's definitely striking, but you don't have anything to worry about with Mac."

Luc gritted his teeth but couldn't stop a groan from escaping as the paramedic-marshal worked on his arm. To distract himself from the stinging pain, he contemplated Priscilla. Her formerly blond hair was now brown with purple and turquoise streaks. Today she wore it in two buns on either side of her head, which meant it was longer than the short haircut she sported the night they'd met. He jerked his thoughts away from wondering how long her hair was. He was here to end their nonexistent marriage, not rekindle a failed romance. A broken engagement right after college and a missing bride had undermined Luc's confidence in sustaining a relationship. His busy work schedule made meeting women difficult, and over the years it became easier to not even try than to have his heart broken again. Both sets of grandparents and his own parents had fairy-tale marriages—the love between each couple had been nauseating to him and his siblings as children, but now it served to highlight his own inability to find someone with whom he could settle down.

Luc bit back a yelp as Grayson used tweezers to extract something from the wound.

"Sorry, got some of the bandanna in the wound."

"That's okay. I'm not usually so sensitive, but today has been anything but normal."

Grayson affixed a fresh bandage on the wound, then wrapped it in gauze. "There, that will keep it covered. Now, time for your shot of antibiotics."

Luc grunted as the man gave the shot.

After adhering a bandage to the injection site, Grayson stripped off his gloves. "You'll be as good as new in no time."

Luc stood. "Are we done here?"

Grayson nodded as he cleaned up the supplies.

"Thanks. I'm going to check on Priscilla." Luc pushed open the kitchen door and hurried into the living room.

Priscilla and Mac stopped talking at his entrance. "How's the arm?" Priscilla gestured toward the fresh bandage.

"Sore." Luc looked from one to the other. "What happens next?"

Mac's eyes hardened.

Luc braced himself for what the marshal would say.

The other man didn't disappoint. "You tell us why you've been following Priscilla."

FIVE

Priscilla frowned as Luc's face paled. His wound looked fine from the outside, but he had lost some blood. Being shot wasn't something one recovered from quickly. Even she was still edgy not knowing for certain the danger had passed. Furthermore, she disagreed with Mac about pressing Luc for answers, but her handler had been firm.

Luc and Mac stood nearly toe to toe, sizing each other up like prizefighters about to start round one. Not good at all. There had been enough blood spilled today.

"Why don't we sit down?" She promptly put action to her words by choosing one end of the sagging brown couch. Luc took the chair to her right while Mac sank onto the love seat perpendicular to the sofa.

Mac immediately addressed Luc. "Mr. Langsdale, why don't we start with some background on who you are?"

"I work for CS Enterprises, a government contractor. My area of expertise is in cybersecurity. Currently, I'm assigned to the US Department of Homeland Security to develop a new protocol for accessing the internet over Wi-Fi that doesn't compromise the security of the data being sent or received."

Priscilla knew little about the ins and outs of cybersecurity, but Luc sounded like someone who could find things out. Like her location. Although why he would want to do so had yet to be answered.

Mac casually pushed his suit coat aside to reveal his holstered weapon, his gaze never leaving Luc's face, which had regained its color. "You know your way around computers."

Luc nodded. "Since I was a kid, I've been fascinated with them." A sheepish grin crossed his face. "I hacked into my dad's email when I was nine just to see if I could do it. It was so easy that I got a little carried away and hacked into my teacher's email, then the principal's. I sent some 'joke' emails that would only be funny to a fourth grader." He rubbed his chin. "But I wasn't as savvy as I thought because I signed the emails with my initials."

Priscilla grinned as a smile surfaced on Mac's face too.

Luc's story broke the tension in the room like water cresting a dam. Her shoulders relaxed for the first time since the shooting. "What happened?"

"I was grounded for a month. Then my dad enrolled me in a code-writing class at the local community college to, as he put it, 'better channel my interest in computers.'" Luc leaned back and crossed his ankle over his knee. "My dad had spoken with the teacher, who agreed to let me attend on a trial basis. I think the teacher thought I would drop out after the first class because it would be too hard for me. But I loved it, and the teacher soon realized I had a knack for writing—and finding flaws in—code."

"In other words, you had hacking skills." Mac let his smile drop.

Luc acknowledged Mac's statement with a nod. "I've

been working on helping companies discern flaws in their supposedly secure platforms since I was a teenager." He tapped his crossed leg with his fingers.

"I see. And now you're working for a Homeland Security contractor. What's your security clearance?" Mac asked in a casual voice that Priscilla knew was anything but casual.

The implication of Luc's ability hit home for Priscilla. If he was that good at hacking, then he probably put those skills to use to find her.

"Top secret."

"Hmm." Mac leaned forward, his gaze sharp. "That type of security clearance would give you access to sensitive government systems and documents."

Luc uncrossed his leg and straightened, his frame tensing. "If you're implying that I used my security clearance to read things I wasn't supposed to, you're wrong."

"I'm not implying." Mac narrowed his eyes. "Did you use your access to find Priscilla?"

"Not exactly."

Mac's eyebrows rose.

Luc held up a hand. "Wait a minute. I didn't do anything illegal. My job was to double-check security measures certain government agencies used to safeguard data. And I also had to see that anyone seeking data on one or two individuals had the same level of security."

Priscilla reflexively reached up to check on the stability of her side hair buns, then jabbed a bobby pin back into one as she listened. She had a feeling she knew what Luc would reveal next.

"I used the name *Priscilla Makin* to check the security levels at a number of government databases." Luc paused.

"But that still doesn't explain *why* you decided to search for that particular name."

Priscilla stiffened at Mac's tone. She was beginning to think there was more to Luc's search of her than he had revealed, and she wasn't sure she was going to like his answers.

"The thing is, I had been looking for Priscilla for a while and getting nowhere." Luc clasped his hands together as he rested his elbows on his knees.

Priscilla frowned. "Why would you be looking for me?"

"Because we know—well, knew—each other." Luc's eyes bored into hers. "And we have unfinished business."

Priscilla searched his face, noting the strong jawline with its slight stubble, the thick golden hair, the vivid blue eyes, the broad shoulders. All of which were very pleasing to look at but brought no spark of remembrance to mind. Surely if she knew him, she would have some memory of him. Only the hours prior to the murders had been blanked from her memory. Doctors called it "selective amnesia" brought on by the traumatic event of Culvert executing three people practically right in front of her. "We did? When? Where?"

Luc's gaze intensified, almost as if he was willing her to recall their acquaintance. "Las Vegas."

"Vegas?" She blinked. "Where?" She tried to puzzle out how she might have known him, sifting through her acquaintances, but coming up short.

"The most recent time was at the Last Chance Casino."

She sucked in a breath. "I worked there once, as a cocktail waitress." That she remembered quite clearly. She'd spent long hours working as a cocktail waitress at the busy Last Chance Casino on the Vegas Strip, trying to save enough to finish her bachelor's degree. Unfortunately, she'd had to leave that part of her life unfinished when she'd entered WITSEC. Since she'd always been interested in hairstyling, the witness protection program had paid for her beautician's license under her new name.

"We met when I went there for a bachelor party for someone I'd known in college. My fiancée had broken up with me over Christmas—we had talked about getting married that summer—so I thought it would help take my mind off my failed engagement." A faint blush stole over his cheeks. "Vegas wouldn't have been my choice, but Brian, the groom, wanted to gamble, drink and flirt with pretty girls—not necessarily in that order—before he got hitched. His words, not mine."

Priscilla shook her head. "I still don't remember you." She frowned in an effort to recall Luc. "There were a lot of bachelor parties."

"Popular place." Luc looked down at his shoes, then up at her. "But you might remember our group because one of our party was the reason you were fired."

Her stomach clenched. She had lost her job the night of the shooting.

"When was this trip of yours?" Mac interjected.

Priscilla had nearly forgotten Mac was listening, her attention laser focused on Luc.

Luc leaned forward. "Seven years ago."

She struggled not to panic. "What day?"

Luc didn't waver his gaze from her face. "June 20."

She closed her eyes and mentally did a free fall into time spent working at the casino. An image of a killer calmly shooting two men and a woman at point-blank range as they pleaded for their lives assailed her. She opened her eyes, blinking back tears.

"I didn't see you." She turned to Mac, her eyes wide. "He wasn't there." Priscilla pointed a trembling finger at Luc. "You weren't in the kitchen, not when that man shot those people!"

"That's enough, Priscilla." Mac touched her arm. "Don't say anything more."

Priscilla swallowed the words on the tip of her tongue, recognizing Mac's warning glare. She had come close to blurting out details that would make it clear that she knew a lot more than anyone outside of a small group of federal marshals and one US attorney had reason to suspect. Her identity had been a close-kept secret, and she had nearly blown her cover in her shock at Luc's words. But how did he recall with such clarity one day over seven years ago?

"I didn't see anyone shoot anyone." Luc's voice held bewilderment. "Who was shot?"

"That's not important right now." Mac snapped out the statement. "Right now, you're telling us how you know Priscilla."

The tension in the room rose along with the hackles on Priscilla's neck. Mac was on edge, maybe because of Luc and his sudden appearance into her life. She had a feeling that Luc could fill in some of the gaps in her memory of that night. Priscilla refocused on ferreting out that information. "You're telling me I served you and your bachelor friends drinks, right?"

Luc kept his attention squarely on Priscilla. The pleading in his eyes tugged at her to remember him.

"Why would that make you search for Priscilla all these years later?" Mac voiced the very question swimming in her own mind.

"Because there's more to the story than my interest in a pretty waitress." Luc drew in a deep breath, and Priscilla braced herself for what was to come. It couldn't be good news, not with this big buildup. What would make a man search for a woman he'd met seven years ago? Then again, she'd known of another cocktail waitress who received a huge tip days after a gambler won the jackpot. The gambler had explained the waitress brought him good luck. But seven years was an awfully long time to hunt someone down to tip.

"I found you crying after your manager fired you." Luc spoke rapidly, as if he had to get everything out at once. "You told me everything—about your needing money to finish school and how your boss threatened to blackball you from all the casinos on the Strip. By the end of your story, I wanted to help you any way I could."

Surely he wasn't saying he'd fallen in love with her. Priscilla had no time for love, not when her every fiber concentrated on staying alive. Shoving that aside to examine when she wasn't running for her life, she instead concentrated on trying to recall the events he talked about, but the shootings had blasted the previous day's memories out of her mind entirely. She didn't remember why she'd been fired. Only a handful of people knew she actually didn't remember the shooting with great detail—just an impression of shots and the shooter's gray eyes devoid of any emotion at all. If he'd seen her in her hiding place underneath a room-service cart, she would have been dead. She had been able to describe his height because of where he stood as he shot the three people, and she would never forget his voice, low, calm, deadly. But she couldn't admit that nearly the entire twenty-four hours preceding the murders were very hazy. "I don't remember much about that night."

Luc frowned. "You're saying that you don't remember anything prior to the shooting?"

"Everything's murky. I have impressions of serving drinks, talking to people, but it's as if it happened behind a gauzy curtain."

Luc sighed. "That explains a lot, and makes this much more difficult than I imagined."

"What's more difficult?"

"I don't know how to say this, so straight out seems the best way." Luc straightened. "I'm your husband."

Priscilla jerked back, shock radiating throughout her body. She surged to her feet. "You're my what?"

Luc stood as well. "Your husband. We're married."

"No, no, no." She shook her head vigorously. "That can't possibly be true." She turned to Mac, who had risen as well. "Mac, how can he say such things?"

"I can assure you that it's true." Luc intervened before Mac could answer her. "I'm sure Mac will find out easily enough that I'm telling the truth."

SIX

The Chinese takeout for dinner earlier had been tasty, but Luc now wished he hadn't overindulged on the Szechuan chicken. He rolled over on the lumpy twin bed in one of the upstairs bedrooms and a mattress spring gouged his back. He couldn't help but wonder if Mac assigned the room knowingly. The marshal had to be aware of Luc's marriage to Priscilla—the other man came across as a by-the-book law-enforcement officer, who would do a thorough background check on anyone getting too close to his witness. Luc had been about to press the matter with the marshal, but the other agent announced dinner had arrived, and Mac suggested the discussion be tabled until later.

Priscilla had only picked at her food, then excused herself to go lie down. Why Mac hadn't confirmed the marriage remained a puzzle, but ferreting his motivation to remain silent would have to be dealt with in the morning.

Of all the scenarios that Luc had thought of when finally face-to-face with Priscilla, he never factored in her utter lack of recognition. It was beyond his comprehension that she would have no memory of their meeting and hasty marriage. If she couldn't recall him, it might make it easier to convince her to sign the annulment papers he'd had a lawyer draw up. All that was needed was both of their signatures on the document to delete their hasty union.

Luc blew out a breath and glanced at the bedside clock, which blinked 12:49 a.m. Maybe something hot to drink would settle his stomach and his mind enough to sleep. He tossed the blanket back and swung his legs over the side of the bed, wincing with the movement. The chilly air made him shiver and he reached for the clean dress shirt that one of the other agents had given him to wear. After donning the shirt, Luc gingerly slipped into his jeans and shoes, then descended to the first floor. He entered the kitchen through the open swing door.

Grayson looked up, a cup of steaming coffee by his elbow and a John Grisham novel in his hand. "Hi, Luc. Need some pain meds?"

At the mention of medication, Luc decided it would be a good idea to get ahead of the pain, even though his arm ached only a little at the moment. "Some ibuprofen would be great." Spotting a Keurig on the counter, he asked, "Got any decaf?"

"In the cupboard above the machine. Mugs too."

Luc selected a pod and popped it in the machine. He then grabbed an I "heart" Coffee mug from the cabinet and spooned sugar into the mug before hitting Start. "Any chance there's real cream?"

"Yeah, in the fridge."

After the coffee dripped in, Luc added the cream, stirred and carried the mug to the table to sit opposite Grayson. "How about that ibuprofen?"

The agent reached into the first-aid kit still sitting

on the table and slid a two-pack of pills across to Luc, who broke the seal and downed the contents. "Thanks."

"You were fortunate the bullet only winged your arm."

"I know." Luc stared into the mug as if the creamy liquid held the secret to getting his life back on track. Now that he'd found Priscilla, he had more questions, and the only answer he'd found was why she'd disappeared all those years ago.

"I couldn't help overhearing your conversation with Mac and Priscilla earlier." Grayson regarded Luc over the rim of his mug before taking a sip and setting the mug on the table. "Mac's top priority is keeping her safe, but he's going to want details on how, exactly, you found her."

Luc sighed. "You mean how I managed to track her down if she's in witness protection?"

"Exactly." Grayson tapped his fingers on the table. "So, how did you?"

"Are you playing good cop?" Luc scrubbed a hand over his jaw, feeling the stubble underneath his fingers.

Grayson laughed. "Maybe, but you'll have to tell us sooner or later."

"And you're saying it might as well be sooner."

Grayson shrugged.

Luc considered, then shrugged himself. "Given you overheard my conversation with Mac and Priscilla, then you know my background in computer security."

Grayson nodded. "You're a hacker for the good guys, finding flaws in their computer security systems."

Luc laughed. "That's one way to put it. Along the way, I've made a lot of contacts with those who are not as concerned with who exactly are the good guys, as you put it. For some, it's the challenge of the job that's interesting, not the goal of the client or what the client will do with the information once the job's completed."

"In other words, you know some unethical people."

"I like to think of it as keeping potential enemies on my good side." Luc took another sip of coffee.

"Is there room for one more?" Priscilla spoke from behind him.

Luc twisted to see her standing in the doorway, fully dressed in clothes as wrinkled as his own. With her face scrubbed free of makeup and her long hair in a messy ponytail, she looked beautiful to Luc. Even her eyes were back to the blue he recalled—she must have removed her colored contact lenses. He didn't care that he was staring—he had forgotten just how lovely she was.

"Sure." Grayson answered her question. "If you want something hot, there are pods in the cabinet above the Keurig."

Priscilla smiled her thanks. Luc admired her easy grace as she walked to the machine. She quickly made a cup and carried it to the kitchen table, easing into the chair to his left.

"Couldn't sleep?" Luc wrapped his hands around his mug.

She smothered a yawn behind her hand. "After the day I've had, it's not too surprising. I did manage to catch a few hours' rest after dinner, but now I can't get back to sleep."

"What's not surprising?" Mac entered the kitchen and headed straight to the Keurig.

"That we couldn't sleep," Luc supplied.

Glass shattered, accompanied by a whooshing sound. "Get down, now!" Mac shouted.

Luc dived out of his chair, his hand shooting out to grab Priscilla's arm to tug her down after him. Luc pushed Priscilla under the table, his hand sliding down her arm to grasp her hand, just as an acrid scent permeated the house.

"The couch is on fire!" Mac yelled into his earpiece to alert the other marshals, then swung shut the kitchen door leading to the dining room before moving to the sink and turning on the faucet. He opened a drawer and yanked out a stack of kitchen towels.

Another crash indicated a second projectile had likely been thrown into the house.

"Put this under the door to buy us some time." Mac tossed Luc a soaked kitchen towel.

Luc let go of Priscilla's hand to catch the towel, then wedged the wet fabric into the crack at the bottom of the door. Once it dried, the smoke would seep into the room again.

"We have to get out of here! I'm going to check the back," Grayson said, crawling to the back door.

"Be careful, Grayson!" Mac called as he handed Priscilla another soaked towel. "Tie this over your nose and mouth."

Grayson slowly pulled open the door. Gunshots erupted and a torrent of bullets shredded the wooden door. Grayson crumpled to the floor in a pool of blood.

Mac shoved a wet towel into Luc's hands, then dropped to his knees beside the downed marshal and placed his fingers on the man's neck. His eyes met Luc's. "He's gone." Mac swallowed hard, then tied his own wet towel over his mouth and nose.

A man was dead, and they would soon follow from smoke inhalation or fire. A little smoke filled the room already. Luc pressed the cold wetness against his nose and mouth as he tied the towel behind his head. Immediately, he breathed a little bit easier, but he could hear the fire roaring behind the kitchen. Priscilla huddled beside him. "Is there another way out?"

Mac's face settled into grim lines. "We could try a back bedroom window."

"There's some kind of hatch underneath the rug in the hallway." Priscilla's eyes watered above her towel. "I tripped on the rug earlier tonight and saw it. Maybe it leads to a crawl space?"

"We can go through that door." Luc pointed to the third entrance into the kitchen a few feet from the table. "I'll check it first." He moved to the door and placed his hand on the wood. Warmish, but not hot. "I think we might have a chance."

Mac grabbed the fire extinguisher from the kitchen wall. "Priscilla, you stay back as Luc pulls open the door. I'll spray the fire if it's too close."

Luc stood to turn the handle. It didn't budge, possibly because the door wasn't used as much as the swing-door entrance. He tried again, this time moving the handle enough to unlatch the door. Bracing his foot against the door frame, Luc tugged with all his might. His arm screamed in agony at the pressure, but the door popped open, nearly sending him tumbling across the kitchen floor.

Fire extinguisher brandished like a sword, Mac went into the hallway first, nearly duckwalking to keep low to the ground. "Come on!"

Priscilla crawled after him, turning to the right, Luc at her heels. She scrabbled to get the rug out of the way, and Luc cried with relief at the sight of a brass ring and the outline of a trapdoor.

He pulled up with his remaining strength, and the door gave way with a groan to reveal a dark space below.

Above her own makeshift mask, Priscilla's eyes widened. Luc touched her arm. "I'll go first."

"No, I'd better check it out." Mac handed Luc the extinguisher. "Spray this at the fire right before you follow Priscilla." Mac swung his legs over and jumped into the space. When he stood up in the opening, his shoulders and head were in the hallway. "It's some sort of crawl space, not a real basement. Let's go!"

Priscilla reached out and Mac put his hands around her waist to swing her down. Luc sprayed the fire extinguisher at the flames racing down the hallway, then joined them. The marshal closed the trapdoor behind him, shutting out the light, but not the smoke or roar of the fire.

As Mac shone his phone's flashlight around the space, Luc saw that it was indeed a crawl space—a haven into which smoke was filtering at an alarming rate.

"Do you see an exit?" Luc focused his attention on examining the area as Mac illuminated their surroundings with a flashlight app.

Embers dropped down around them from the burning floor above, one of them singeing his cheek, but Luc's attention fixated on the spot Mac's light had just passed over. "Shine it to the right again." Mac complied. "There's a narrow opening to the left of us."

"Let's move." Mac gestured for Luc to go first, then Priscilla.

In tandem, they crawled in that direction, still using the rapidly drying towels to screen out smoke. Above the roar of the fire, sirens wailed. Maybe they would survive this night after all.

At the opening, Mac turned to Luc. "You go first to make sure it's safe. I need to stick close to Priscilla. Help is coming, but we can't wait here until it arrives.

Be careful. We don't know how many might be out there waiting for us."

Luc pushed aside a few vines that covered the entrance and wriggled out from under the house. The heat from the fire told him they didn't have much time. He scanned the area but saw no movement. Fire trucks roared up to the house. "I think it's okay. Come on, Priscilla."

She reached out her hand and Luc grasped it to assist her exit from the crawl space. Soon she was hiding in the bushes with him, waiting for Mac to emerge.

Once Mac joined them, he pointed to the backyard of the neighboring house that had a thatch of bamboo growing along the border. "Over there."

Mac led the way as Luc and Priscilla followed close behind him. Once standing just inside the bamboo stand, Mac pulled out his phone, shielding the bright light with his body to avoid tipping off anyone watching the house. "I sent a text to let headquarters know what happened."

Luc evaluated the burning house about fifteen feet away. Firefighters swarmed in the front yard, hoses spraying the flames with little success.

"We need to get moving." Mac slipped his phone back into a pocket. "We'll go through the backyards to the street on the other side. My boss is sending a car to pick us up there."

Luc grabbed Priscilla's hand. He wasn't sure why he wanted to hold on to her, but he had to. She didn't say a word or look in his direction as they dashed after Mac through the backyards, then through a side alleyway.

Mac halted at the corner, checking his phone again. "Our ride's here." An SUV pulled up to the alleyway's entrance. Mac motioned for them to precede him to the vehicle. "Get in the back."

Luc reached it first and opened the door. Priscilla slid inside, Luc right behind her. Mac slammed the door on the passenger side and the vehicle took off before anyone had their seat belt buckled.

"You okay?" A woman in her early thirties drove.

"It was a close one, Ilene." Mac fixed his attention on his phone.

"There's bottled water in the cup holders," Ilene said, heading down the street.

Luc uncapped one of the bottles and took a long draw to soothe his parched throat. "Thanks." He leaned toward Priscilla, who was recapping her bottle. "Hey," he said softly, "how are you holding up?"

She shrugged. "I've been better, but I don't think I'm really hurt. You?"

"Smoky, but in one piece." Luc wanted to recapture her hand in his, but decided to listen to Ilene's update to Mac instead.

"We're heading to a clinic to check everyone out before driving to another safe location. One of the doctors we've worked with before is opening the clinic just for us." Ilene turned left. "We should arrive in ten minutes."

"Has it been checked out?" Mac questioned.

Ilene nodded. "A pair of agents are clearing it now, and it will be secure before we arrive."

Luc rested his head against the seat, tired, dirty, but thankful to be alive. Since meeting up with Priscilla again, life had been anything but dull. As they drove down the street, Luc recalled that the burning house they'd just left had been cleared by marshals too.

SEVEN

The nurse in dark green scrubs with small red holiday wreaths, whose name Priscilla had already forgotten, reentered the curtained-off exam room. "I need to draw some blood to check your red blood cell count."

Priscilla nodded and leaned back against the raised examining bed. She breathed in oxygen through a mask the nurse had placed on her earlier. The diminutive woman's youthful appearance belied her competent manner. The nurse placed a squishy ball in Priscilla's left hand, then fastened rubber tubing around her upper arm.

"Just a small prick now."

Despite the fact that the nurse had hit the blood vessel spot-on, Priscilla winced as the needle entered her vein. Not wanting to see her blood being drawn, she closed her eyes.

Although her lungs were much better from the extra oxygen, her head still ached. She wanted to sleep for a full day, but that would be a long time coming. Once she, Mac and Luc had been checked out at the clinic, the marshals would take her and Luc to a new safe house.

"All done." The nurse undid the tubing and removed the ball.

Priscilla opened her eyes, even though fatigue pulled

at her eyelids and the drums in her head began a more up-tempo number.

"If you'll hold this in place?" The nurse put a small piece of gauze over the needle.

"Sure." Priscilla put her fingers over the gauze as the nurse slid the needle out.

"Okay, let me check." The woman assessed the clotting, then replaced the gauze with a fresh square before wrapping it in place with green bandage tape. She made a notation on a clipboard and patted Priscilla's hand. "You rest for a minute. The doctor's taking a look at your friend's arm. Then he'll be in to see you."

She nodded, but allowed her eyes to close as the nurse left the area. Maybe she could catch a few minutes' sleep, despite the pounding in her head. But while her body sagged after the adrenaline rush of escaping a burning house, her mind raced with thoughts about being married to Luc. How could she be married to a man she didn't remember meeting? They must have met and wed within a four- or five-hour time period. She had never been that impulsive in her life. Luc hadn't said anything about love at first sight either. Why had he married a complete stranger?

Granted, strange things happened in Vegas. She'd grown up an only child in a close suburb with a stay-at-home mother and a father who brought back tales of the city's seedier side from his observations as a beat cop. Priscilla had worked in the casinos since she turned eighteen—the best-paid job she could find with a high school diploma—and she had seen firsthand what alcohol, gambling and an atmosphere of "anything goes" could produce. Even though Mac hadn't confirmed the marriage, Priscilla didn't think Luc had been lying.

What their being married meant, she couldn't contemplate. Not when she was running for her life.

The sound of the curtain being pulled back penetrated her consciousness, and Priscilla pried open her eyes. A baby-faced man with curly dark hair and rimless glasses stepped in, a stethoscope looped around his neck.

As he tugged the curtain back in place, he said, "Hi, I'm Doctor Collins. How are you feeling?"

Priscilla removed the oxygen mask. "Better, but my throat hurts, my eyes are itchy, and my head aches a lot."

"Smoke inhalation will do that to a person. Let's have a listen to your lungs and heart." Dr. Collins put his stethoscope against her chest. "Take slow breaths, not too deep."

Priscilla breathed as instructed.

"Your lungs sound clear, and your heart rate is within the normal limit." Dr. Collins put his stethoscope into his lab coat pocket. "On a scale of one to ten, where does your headache fall?"

"Nine maybe? It's sliding into the migraine realm." Priscilla pressed her temples as the pounding morphed into jackhammering inside her skull.

"That's because of the carbon dioxide you inhaled." He poked his head out and called for assistance. Priscilla expected the younger nurse to return, but this time, an older woman wearing dark green scrubs with little dogs romping around on the smock entered the cubicle.

"Martha, would you please bring me 600 milligrams of ibuprofen and a bronchodilator inhaler?" Dr. Collins requested.

The nurse nodded and disappeared.

Dr. Collins turned back to Priscilla. "The ibuprofen should take care of your headache, and the bronchodilator will ease the muscles around your airways to relieve any coughing or shortness of breath you may experience because of the smoke inhalation. The best thing for you is to rest, though. Any questions?"

"When should I use the inhaler?" Priscilla hoped she wouldn't have to use it at all.

"It's a precaution in case you start coughing more later on tonight." He glanced at his watch. "Or this morning, as it's now 2:00 a.m."

"I only use the inhaler if I cough a lot."

"Yes, that's right."

"Thank you, Doctor." She wanted to ask about Mac and Luc, but the man smiled at her, then left the cubicle before she could.

Martha returned with a pill cup in one hand and cup of water in the other. "Here you go."

Priscilla smiled her thanks and tossed back the tablets, then drained the water. "Are Mac and Luc ready to go?"

The nurse shrugged and took back both cups. "I don't know. I'll check."

"That would be great."

As the woman left the cubicle, she drew the curtain partially closed.

"Priscilla? Can I come in?" Luc's voice had a scratchy tone to it, but he sounded much more upbeat than she felt.

"Yes."

The curtain twitched and Luc poked his head around, then entered the cubicle. "How are you feeling?" He sported a scrubbed face, loose navy scrubs, and a fresh white bandage on his upper left arm poking out from under the short sleeve.

Priscilla slid off the bed and steadied herself against the railing. "Like I breathed in a ton of smoke. How about you?" She assessed him, noting the tired lines around his eyes and damp hair.

"The doctor let me shower. Then he rebandaged my arm."

"You got a shower? I'm jealous." She picked at her soot-covered jeans. "Maybe I can grab one too."

Mac joined Luc in the cubicle. "I think that can be arranged." He too was dressed in borrowed scrubs, a bandage on his forehead where he had scraped it during their escape from the crawl space. "Ilene's scrounging up something for you to wear. Then she'll stand guard while you get cleaned up."

"Are we going to another safe house?" Priscilla leaned back against the bed. Man, she was tired. She wanted to collapse in a puddle on the floor, but the thought of washing some of the smoke from her body and hair kept her upright.

"Still working on that." Mac fiddled with his phone. "We should have a destination by the time you're ready to go."

Ilene entered, another set of scrubs in her hand. "I think these will do for now. Ready for that shower?"

Priscilla nodded and followed Ilene into the women's locker area, where the female staff showered and stored their street clothes.

Ilene stopped in front of a cubicle that held a small changing area, then a shower beyond that. "There's soap and shampoo, with a couple of towels in there. Leave your clothes on the floor, and I'll bag them. We should be able to wash them at the next safe house."

"Thanks." After cleaning up, she wrapped her hair in a towel, turban style, and put on the clean clothes Ilene had left for her.

The navy scrubs fit well enough, although she had

to cinch the drawstring tight to avoid having droopy drawers. She shivered in the short sleeves. Hopefully, Ilene had found a coat or sweater to wear too. Priscilla pulled on fresh socks, then shoved her feet back into her black flats. Hanging the towel over the shower rod, she adjusted her hair towel more securely around her head and exited the cubicle.

The locker room was quiet. Frowning, Priscilla poked her head into the other shower stalls but no Ilene. The toilets had no one there either. A shiver of unease coiled around her shoulders.

Ilene shouldn't have left her alone—Mac expected the female marshal to stick close by, so where was she?

A row of tall lockers stood opposite the bank of showers. Priscilla eased toward them, her heart rate accelerating. What if Ilene was stuffed inside a locker? She was letting her imagination and the events of the previous twelve hours make her paranoid.

Priscilla turned just in time to see the outline of someone raising a blunt object over her head.

"Nooo!" Priscilla raised her arms to defend against the attack, but the blow struck hard and she crumpled to the floor.

EIGHT

Luc tossed the weeks-old *People* magazine back onto the pile on a table in the clinic's small waiting room. Mac had disappeared into an office with two of the four marshals who had arrived while Priscilla was showering. The other two patrolled the exterior of the building.

After all that had happened, he didn't like to let Priscilla out of his sight. If Mac trusted Ilene to keep her safe, Luc knew he should be able to do the same.

Should being the operative word. He should be able to let the marshals do their job. But something didn't feel right. He'd overheard enough from Mac and the other agents last night to piece together the facts. Priscilla had seen someone commit murder, and that precipitated her entry into the witness protection program. The suspect—Cuthbert or Culvert—had escaped custody, evidently to silence Priscilla for good. Luc wasn't sure why the man would risk trying to kill Priscilla when he would have known the marshals would step up their security given his escape, but the marshals hadn't mentioned anyone else who would want Priscilla dead.

A glance at the wall clock revealed twenty minutes had elapsed since Ilene and Priscilla entered the women's locker room. He would check on them. The quiet, dimly lit hallway made the hairs on the back of his neck stand to attention. His sneakers squeaked on the shiny floor as he approached the sign indicating the women's locker room. He placed his hand on the door handle, then paused.

This was ridiculous, checking up on Priscilla when a US marshal was her bodyguard, yet he couldn't shake the feeling that something was wrong. If he entered and Ilene reprimanded him, so be it. He could stand a little embarrassment to put his unease to rest, and perhaps Priscilla wouldn't be too embarrassed for his bursting in.

Squaring his shoulders, he knocked, then pulled open the door and entered. Silence greeted him. He stopped in the L-shaped curve that kept the changing areas hidden from the outside door. He listened intently. Luc inched up to the top of the L and peered around the corner. A movement at the far end of the locker room caught his eye.

"Marshal?" He approached the area and spotted Priscilla lying in a heap, partially hidden by one of the benches. He dropped to his knees beside her, resisting the urge to gather her into his arms. Instead, he reached down and touched his fingers lightly to her neck. Her heartbeat pulsed beneath his fingers and her eyelids fluttered. Luc sighed in relief.

He rocked back on his heels to further assess her, but instantly sensed a presence behind him.

"Keep your hands where I can see them." The marshal spoke over his left shoulder.

Luc raised his hands. "Ilene, what happened?"

The woman rounded the bench. "What did you do to Ms. Anderson?" Her Glock was aimed at his chest.

"Me? I didn't do anything. I came to check on you two and found her like this. Where were you?" Luc didn't lower his hands. "Priscilla's hurt. She needs medical attention."

Ilene held the gun steady with one hand and pulled her cell phone out with the other. She hit a button before holding the phone to her ear. "Mac? Send the doctor to the women's locker room. Something's happened to Priscilla."

She slipped the phone back into her pocket. "Now, step away from her slowly and keep your hands raised."

Without objecting, Luc scrambled to his feet, his hands reaching for the ceiling, and moved back from the still form on the floor.

"Sit on that bench and don't move." Ilene tipped her head in the direction of one of the benches.

As Luc lowered his body gingerly onto the wooden bench, the outer door opened, and Mac, followed by Dr. Collins, rushed in. Ignoring Luc, the pair hurried over to Priscilla. Luc tried to follow exactly what the doctor said to Mac about Priscilla, but the distance and the distraction of Ilene standing with her gun pointed directly at him made concentrating difficult.

Two more agents entered the locker room, conferred briefly with Mac and began searching the area.

"Do you think you can put that away?" Luc appealed to Ilene. "I'd never hurt Priscilla."

Ilene eyed him, then holstered her weapon. "Do. Not. Move."

"Yes, ma'am." Luc wrapped his fingers around the edge of the bench, angling his body to see what was happening. Dr. Collins still bent over her, but Luc could see she was alert and appeared to be answering his questions.

Ilene, her eyes never leaving Luc, stood to the side with Mac.

Luc nearly wept with relief when Priscilla sat up and discarded her hair towel. She was okay. The doctor said something to her and she replied, but Luc could hear only the beating of his heart in thanksgiving for her safety.

Mac walked over to him, his expression grim.

"What happened?" Luc stood. "Will she be okay?"

"Dr. Collins said she suffered a blow to the head but her hair wrapped up in a towel absorbed much of the blow. As a result, she was only stunned. Exhaustion fed into her unresponsiveness." Mac had his phone out. "We'll need to keep an eye on her, but it looks like she'll be okay."

"Who hit her? And why did Ilene leave her alone?" Luc had been tired but this third close call with Priscilla spiked his adrenaline again. He wanted to be doing something.

"We don't know." Mac shook his head. "Ilene said that she received an urgent text purportedly from her daughter's nanny. She stepped outside the locker room to make a phone call. Cell phone reception isn't great in here for long phone calls."

Luc frowned. "But she wasn't here when I—"

"She had to walk around the corner, but kept an eye on the outer door, which was why she spotted you entering."

The wheels spun in Luc's mind, and he played out the scenario. "Then how did whoever hit Priscilla get inside?"

"Looks like a window over one of the toilets has been jimmied open." Mac's expression remained hard.

"They were locked, but a professional wouldn't have had any trouble gaining access," Ilene interjected.

Another marshal joined them to report. "The premises are cleared, and no footprints on the ground outside the windows in this locker room. The outside security cameras don't cover the back side of the building."

"Thanks." Mac glanced at his phone. "We'll leave in five. Tell the others." He slipped his phone back into his pocket as Dr. Collins and Priscilla walked up. "How are you feeling?"

"My head hurts. Again." Priscilla's smile wobbled on her lips. Her skin hadn't regained its color, leaving her looking frail.

Dr. Collins patted her shoulder. "I'll send some acetaminophen with you for the pain, but you need to wait a few hours before taking it. The nurse will give you an ice pack. Place it on for twenty minutes, then off for ten, repeating as necessary to help reduce the swelling on the contusion."

Mac interjected, "Got our destination. We'll be leaving in a couple of minutes."

"Are you sure Priscilla's ready to travel?" Luc fought the urge to wrap her up in his arms and tell her everything would be okay. He wanted only to see her to safety to discuss what happened seven years ago.

"I'll be all right." Priscilla flipped a wet strand of hair over her shoulder, but Luc thought he detected more bravado behind the gesture, as if she was pretending to be fine. "I can rest in the car."

Luc frowned. "Shouldn't you stay awake because of the bump on the head?"

"She has a small contusion above her left ear, but since her towel turban absorbed most of the blow, she didn't suffer from a concussion," Dr. Collins explained.

"But she passed out. Wouldn't that mean she was hit harder than that?" Luc glanced at Priscilla, who had loosely braided her hair and now fastened a hair tie at the end.

"I think that was due more to her body being on overload from the events of the past day. In other words, she was exhausted, and it only took a little push for her body to shut down." Dr. Collins regarded Luc. "She'll be okay. Trust me on this."

Mac consulted his phone. "Ride's here. Let's go."

Luc followed them through the clinic. At the door, a nurse handed Priscilla a bag with her medicine. As they stepped out into the night, Luc shot a prayer heavenward. *Thank You for keeping Priscilla safe. Please let the marshals find the person responsible before any more harm comes to her.*

In the back seat of yet another SUV, Priscilla leaned her head against the seat. Mac occupied the seat beside her, while another marshal drove. Luc rode in a separate vehicle behind theirs. A third SUV with two agents led the way. While glad to be able to rest for a while during the trip to a second secure location, she missed Luc's presence. Even though Mac had made no bones about the fact that he wasn't entirely sure Luc's entry into her life hadn't triggered these incidents, she didn't feel threatened by Luc. Why she would feel that way after so short a time, she didn't have the brain power to contemplate. Her eyes slid closed, and Priscilla used the quiet to thank God for keeping her safe over the past twenty-four hours.

"Praying?"

Priscilla blinked and straightened in the seat. Mac glanced at her, his cell phone in his hand.

"Seemed like the right thing to do." Priscilla didn't apologize or explain why, just stated it as a fact. Mac had seen her pray often over the years he had been assigned as her contact.

"You pray more than anyone I've ever known." Mac placed a hand on her arm. "We'll get this guy. I can promise you that."

Priscilla summoned a smile. "I know you'll try your hardest, Mac."

Mac turned the screen off on his cell. "I suppose that means you think God might have other plans."

"He might." Priscilla didn't preach Christianity to Mac, but instead preferred to live her faith and let that speak for itself.

"Forgive me for saying so, but that sounds ominous." He turned to her and raised his eyebrows. "You haven't changed your mind about what you said when we met the first time, have you?"

"Refresh my memory?"

Mac drew in a breath and let it out in a whoosh. "You once told me that if Culvert managed to kill you despite my best efforts, I wasn't to take it personally—that sometimes our plans differ from God's plans."

Priscilla chose her words carefully. Mac didn't often bring up her faith, although she wasn't shy about who she knew to be in charge of the universe. "God calls each of his children home in different ways. Mine might be at the hands of a murderer or it might be in my sleep at a ripe old age. But however it happens, I know that it will be for God's glory and for my good."

"How can you believe that death at the hands of a murderer is part of God's plan for you?" Mac's gaze intensified, as if willing her to say the words to erase his own doubts about God. "Someone is trying to kill you. A man you can't remember says he's your husband. And you're telling me that your faith is so solid, so sure, that a bullet between your eyes would be for the glory of your God."

Since his assignment to guard her after she'd been in WITSEC for four years, she'd learned that his faith was in himself, in his ability to weather any storm life sent his way. Now Priscilla answered him with confidence, knowing that Mac could easily dismiss the truth like he'd done over the past three years.

"It's God's peace." As she spoke, that peace settled deep into her own heart, strengthening her resolve and faith. "For me, I know I'm in the palm of His hand and that nothing of this world can truly hurt me."

Mac's perplexed expression softened. He opened his mouth to speak, but before he could respond, his cell phone buzzed. "Mac." He sobered as he listened to the caller. "I see. When?"

Whoever was on the other end had delivered bad news—she was sure of that by Mac's posture and clipped words.

Mac kept his attention on Priscilla in the dim interior of the car. "He's getting more desperate." After a few more exchanges, he disconnected.

"What happened?"

"Trevor Grammar has been killed."

"Grammar? One of the other witnesses scheduled to appear at Culvert's trial?"

Mac nodded. "Marshals found him a few hours ago dead and the word *snitch* written on the wall beside him."

Her breath came out in a gasp. "That's terrible."

"Grammar refused to enter the witness protection program and didn't even want any bodyguards." Mac rubbed his face. "It was his right to refuse, but we repeatedly warned him of the danger, and had contacted him again when Culvert escaped."

Mac delivered the news to the marshals in the front seat, then called the men in the other vehicles. Beside him, Priscilla tried to regulate her own breathing, not wanting to let her dismay over Grammar's murder send her into a panic. As a middleman between Culvert and his clients, Grammar had brokered assignments with high-profile targets. Grammar's direct knowledge of Culvert's career as a hit man had helped the US attorney build a bigger case against Culvert beyond the casino shootings she'd witnessed. She had faith that could move mountains—wasn't that what she'd just shared with Mac?

The SUV sped into the brightening sky as the sun awakened from its nightly slumber. Priscilla clung to the promises each new day brought, and prayed that she would live to see the sun go down that evening.

NINE

Luc buttoned the black-and-red flannel shirt, glad for the warmer shirt to combat the crisp early-December day. At least this fit better than the borrowed scrubs from the clinic. He yawned. Despite sleeping for eight hours in the new safe house tucked into a quiet neighborhood a few blocks off the main street in Evans, West Virginia, he hadn't wanted to get up. But Marshal Bill Myers—a huge bald man—had knocked on his door a half hour ago with a sack of clean clothes and an announcement that dinner would be ready in forty-five minutes.

The scent of tomato sauce and oregano beckoned and his stomach growled in reply. A feminine laugh drew him quickly down the hallway to the kitchen, but instead of Priscilla in the kitchen, a couple stood side by side at the counter. A man wearing a University of West Virginia hoodie snitched a piece of carrot from a cutting board while a tall, dark-haired woman in tailored jeans and a navy sweater swatted his hand, a kitchen knife in her other hand.

Disappointment coursed through his veins, but he tamped it down, not wanting to dwell on why he wanted to see Priscilla. He should focus instead on how to broach the subject of what they should do when she couldn't re-member their wedding.

The pair must have sensed his presence because they turned in unison to the doorway. The man popped the carrot in his mouth and crunched, while the woman laid the knife on the counter and held out her hand. "You must be Luc. I'm Marshal Laura Devins, and this rascal is my husband, Dr. Steven Devins, who's a consultant for the US Marshals Service."

Luc shook their hands, then moved back to the door-way. "Where's Mac?"

"He got called back to headquarters, but will return tomorrow morning." She smiled at him. "Don't worry—there are four agents patrolling outside, two more in the house, plus myself and Steven."

Luc relaxed his shoulders. Surely all those highly trained men and women would keep them safe. He sniffed the air as his stomach rumbled more insistently. "Smells good."

"Oh, it will be—it's my grandmother's special spa-ghetti sauce recipe. From the old country." Laura picked up her knife to finish chopping carrots.

"If by old country, you mean Philly, then yes, that's true." Dr. Devins touched his wife's shoulder as he squeezed past her to join Luc near the open door. "Come on—I'll introduce you to the house agents while she finishes the salad."

"What is this, the 1950s? Why aren't you helping?" Laura called after him.

"I thought you didn't want my help!" her husband teased back as he led Luc to the living room, where a slender African American man sat on a worn leather couch tossing cards into an upside-down baseball hat. Seated on a matching love seat, Marshal Myers leaned back with the sleeves of his dress shirt rolled up to reveal a dragon tattoo covering most of his left forearm and a rose encircled with thorns on his right arm. Definitely not what Luc thought a US marshal would look like, but if he kept Priscilla safe, Luc didn't care how many tattoos he had.

Dr. Devins stopped beside the couch. "This is Luc, who got caught up in this mess with Priscilla." Myers and the other man rose as Dr. Devins introduced Marshal Aaron Aldrich.

Aldrich shook Luc's hand, sizing him up. Luc resisted the urge to explain his relationship with Priscilla under their scrutiny.

"Steven?" Laura appeared in the kitchen doorway.

"Coming, love." With a wink, Dr. Devins disappeared into the kitchen.

"Those two make me sick." Myers's smile took the sting out of his words.

Aldrich raised his eyebrows. "Only because he's happily married, and you can't seem to find any woman to go out with your ugly self."

"That may be, but at least I try." Myers retook his seat. "You've given up on love after Darcy broke your heart."

Aldrich chuckled as he sat down, his relaxed demeanor showing he didn't take Myers's remark seriously. "Pay no attention to him and his sob stories, Luc. He's just sore because I beat him in rummy earlier. Now he won't play another hand with me. I'm reduced to tossing cards into a hat for entertainment."

Luc grinned and took the opposite chair. "You two must be partners."

Myers nodded. "How did you know?"

"You're bickering like unhappily married folk." Luc

settled back into the battered club chair. "Is Priscilla awake?"

"Yes." Priscilla spoke from the archway that led to the bedrooms. Her hair twisted up into a loose topknot made her look even younger.

He gestured to his outfit. "We could be twins." Priscilla's clothes echoed his: jeans, white Converse sneakers and a loose-fitting flannel shirt.

When she smiled, his heart squeezed inside his chest, but he ignored the feeling. Better to concentrate on finding who was behind these attacks so he and Priscilla could discuss the best way to end their quickie marriage.

"I suspect someone went shopping at the hunter's outlet store." She stepped farther into the living room. "Hi, Myers, Aldrich. Nice to see you again."

"Wish it were under better circumstances." Aldrich retrieved the cards from the hat and reshuffled.

"Did I interrupt your card game?" Priscilla sank onto the couch next to Aidrich.

"Nah, I beat him earlier, so he quit," Aldrich countered.

"Dinner's ready," Laura called from the kitchen.

Throughout the meal, Luc said little, but his eyes frequently strayed to Priscilla as she exchanged stories with the marshals and teased Aldrich and Myers about their lackluster love lives. After dinner ended, Priscilla said she would take care of the dishes, and Luc immediately volunteered to help.

In the kitchen, she washed and he dried, as the dishwasher was on the fritz. He didn't savor the domesticity of the scene, as he might have if they had a real marriage, but instead wondered how he could bring up the idea of an annulment.

"Penny for your thoughts?" Priscilla cocked her head as she handed him a glass to dry.

Without thinking, Luc blurted out a version of the truth. "I was thinking of how many married couples wash dishes together."

Priscilla bit her lip, her eyes troubled.

He should have kept his mouth shut.

"I'm sorry, Luc." Her gaze slid away from his to stare down into the soapy water. "I don't remember you, let alone marrying you."

She swished the water around and pulled a plate out, dipping it into the rinse water and stacking it in the drainer. "You know what's strange? This morning, while I slept, I did dream of a wedding."

He tried to act casual, but inwardly, he couldn't help but be excited. Hopefully, this would lead to remembering him. While it might be easier to ask for an annulment if she didn't remember their wedding, pushing for it now smacked of taking advantage of the situation. He nodded encouragement, not trusting that he wouldn't say something to break her train of thought.

Priscilla wrinkled her brow as she scrubbed another plate. "I was there, not in a white dress, though. I'm not sure if it was my wedding or not. But there were white roses and Elvis. Not young Elvis, but the rhinestone-jumpsuit version." She shrugged and stacked the plate in the drainer. "How silly is that?"

Luc sucked in a breath and concentrated on not over-reacting. *Stay calm.* His heart pounded, but he managed to say in a low voice, "Was he singing 'Love Me Tender'?"

Her hands stopped cleaning the plate. "How did you—"

"That was our wedding."

That brought her head up with a snap, shock rimming her eyes. "What?"

"We got married in the Graceland Wedding Chapel." He swallowed past the lump of emotion clogging his throat, the thought that maybe this was a breakthrough that would lead to their having a real discussion about their future. "An Elvis impersonator presided over the ceremony." His lips twisted with a smile. "Or, I should say, Jumpsuit Elvis did."

Priscilla's entire body stilled.

Luc kept his voice steady as he added, "He sang 'Love Me Tender' after he pronounced us husband and wife."

Priscilla stared at Luc, her hands holding the plate she'd been about to wash suspended over the suds. Her dream wasn't a dream at all but a memory! Were the bricks at last coming down from the wall her subconscious had erected after witnessing the shootings?

The plate plopped back into the sink, shooting bubbles into the air like confetti. "That was us? You were the one beside me?" She couldn't slow the revved emotions in her body any more than a blow-dryer set on high. "I've had that dream off and on for years, but never saw the groom's face or even thought it was my wedding."

Despite the soapy water, Luc took her hands in his and gave them a light squeeze. "I am relieved to know you didn't completely block out everything from that night."

"You make it sound like I did it on purpose." She pulled her hands away and plunged them back into the water to grab another plate. His tone might not have been accusatory, but his words still rankled.

"I didn't 'block out' anything—I saw something so

horrifying, I haven't been able to remember all the details of that night or the hours before the shootings." She rinsed the plate and stopped herself from slamming it into a slot in the drainer.

Luc spread his hands, palms up, in a conciliatory gesture. "Priscilla, I didn't mean to imply…"

While washing the last plate, she plowed over his words. "Maybe not, but you seem to think that I should be overjoyed to see you, and by merely telling me we're married, I should fall into your arms." She set the plate into the drainer and pulled the plugs in the double sink.

"No, that's not true." He held out the towel to her.

"I think it is." She snatched it and dried her hands. It felt good to let some of the anger and fear over the situation with Culvert spill over.

She tossed the towel on the counter. "How did you find me? I know you said a bunch of stuff about knowing where to look, *blah, blah, blah*. But since you appeared, I've been shot at, nearly set on fire, and hit on the head." She planted her hands on her hips, her voice rising. "How do I know you didn't bring Culvert's attention to me? That he didn't find me because of your searches?"

"That's a very good question." Mac offered a tight smile from the kitchen doorway. "One that we're looking into."

Priscilla reined in her emotions with several deep breaths. "I didn't think you'd be back until tomorrow morning."

Mac pushed his sunglasses up on top of his head as he assessed her with a sweep of his eyes. "You look better than when I dropped you off here at 6:00 a.m."

"I feel better. Not quite back to my old self, but better." She flicked a glance at Luc, then voiced a question that had been burning in her mind since Luc's initial revelation that he was her husband. "Have you found out whether he's even telling the truth about us being married?"

Mac reached into the inner pocket of his suit jacket and extracted a folded piece of paper. "That was one thing I had the office double-check. With the time difference, it took a little longer to get an official copy of the marriage license."

She took the paper and unfolded it, scanning it quickly, then reread more slowly. Her real name, Priscilla Ann Makin, and signature scrawled across the bottom silenced the misgivings in her mind. Luc's slash of a signature underneath his own name left no doubt this man was her husband. "We really did get married." She read the location again. "In Las Vegas, the day before the shooting."

Mac nodded. "And we got the results of a background check on Luc. He is who he says he is."

"Gee, thanks for the vote of confidence after confirming it in black and white." Luc crossed his arms over his chest.

Priscilla wouldn't apologize for Mac and the marshals doing their job, not after all that had happened over the past twenty-four hours. "They have to check, to keep me and other witnesses safe."

"I know." Luc blew out a disgusted breath, as if the fight had drained out of him like the water swirling down the sink. "I think I'll go read for a bit, then hit the hay early. I'm still pretty wiped out."

Priscilla refused to make any attempt to stop him. When he had gone, she sighed. "I'm glad he checked out, given that we're married and all, but I still don't like the coincidence of his showing up and my life turning upside down. I liked my last job. I had friends. Things had been calm even before the FBI had captured Culvert eighteen months ago."

"It does seem a bit improbable to have Culvert escape custody and Luc run into you in close proximity, but from what we've been able to determine, Luc's story checks out." Mac nodded to the wedding license she held in her hand. "I'm going to need to hold on to that until things are resolved."

"Of course." She handed it back, sadness creeping over her at yet another example of her unorthodox life. She couldn't keep anything in her old name, anything that would tie her to her old life. If she still had that life, she'd be married and probably have a few kids underfoot by now. Tears welled and she blinked rapidly to clear her vision as well as to strengthen her resolve. She'd cried enough tears over what wasn't to be, and she wasn't going to shed any more. "I think I'll go to my room too. It's been an eventful day."

"That's probably a good idea. I'll be back to see you tomorrow afternoon."

Priscilla paused in the kitchen doorway. "You're not staying?"

Mac shook his head. "I've got another case that we're preparing for trial. I have to be in the office in the morning for a meeting. Don't worry—Laura, Myers and Aldrich will remain on the premises. There are also marshals monitoring the perimeter of the house. You'll be well covered."

"That's what we thought at the last safe house." Priscilla shuddered at the memory of the fire exploding in the living room and their narrow escape through the crawl space.

"Try to get some sleep." Mac didn't even try to contradict her, merely patted her shoulder before she walked down the hallway to the bedroom next to Luc's.

Priscilla couldn't help but wonder if she would even live long enough to find out if she liked being married or not.

TEN

Luc punched down his pillow but the readjustment of its shape did little to lull him to sleep. The bedside digital clock clicked over to 11:35. The emotional roller coaster he'd been on since reconnecting with Priscilla had drained him. He'd soared hearing Priscilla describe part of their wedding. Then his hopes plummeted to learn just how limited her recall was. Her distrust of his motives also hit him in the gut, although his mind told him she was right to wonder if the events of the past two days had any connection to him.

He rolled onto his back and stared into the darkness. How would they ever be able to discuss ending a marriage that never really got started with a houseful of marshals and a killer on the loose?

There would be no more sleep for a while. He might as well get up. Maybe playing cards with Aldrich and Myers would burn off some of this energy and help him wind down enough to fall asleep. Luc tossed back the bedding, then grabbed the clothes he'd strewn over the back of the chair and dressed.

In the living room, Aldrich sat on the couch dealing a hand of cards to Dr. Devins, who occupied the club chair. The pair looked up at Luc's entrance.

"Couldn't sleep?" Dr. Devins picked up his cards.

"Too much on my mind." Luc sank onto the love seat. "Rummy?"

Aldrich grinned. "It's the only game in town. We'll deal you in next hand."

"Thanks." Luc stretched as the doctor discarded an eight of spades. "What kind of doctor are you?"

"He's the kind that messes with your head." Aldrich snapped up the eight of spades, then laid out a spread with three eights.

"Aldrich meant I'm a psychiatrist."

"Are you messing with mine?" Luc watched a few more minutes of play in silence.

"Smoked you again." Aldrich put down a run, then discarded his last card.

Dr. Devins threw down his hand in disgust. "How do you do that?"

"I was a card shark in another life." Aldrich scooped up the cards and shuffled.

"That I believe." Dr. Devins smiled. "Maybe with Luc playing, I'll do better."

"Wishful thinking." Aldrich dealt Luc into the game.

As the trio gathered their cards, Dr. Devins said, "We were shamelessly listening in on your conversation with Priscilla. She didn't remember many details about your wedding, did she?"

"Or about you." Aldrich stacked the remaining cards and flipped the top one over.

Luc raised his eyebrows but didn't comment. He arranged his cards as if the words hadn't stung. No man liked to think he was forgettable.

Dr. Devins started the hand by drawing a card. "Confession. Besides wanting to spend time with my lovely wife, Mac asked me to come along because of my sub-specialty." He discarded a ten of hearts.

Just the card Luc wanted to go with the jack and nine of hearts. "What's that?" He picked up the ten and laid down his spread, before adding a three of clubs to the discard pile.

"Hypnotherapy." Dr. Devins regarded Luc over his cards. "I've had good success with helping people remember clearer details about events surrounding a traumatic episode in their lives, whether it's the death of a loved one, an accident or, in a few cases, a violent crime."

Luc ignored Aldrich's play, his attention riveted on Dr. Devins. "You're saying you can help Priscilla remember by hypnotizing her?"

"It's possible." Dr. Devins nodded to the cards on the table. "Your turn."

Luc glanced at the discard pile, but didn't need the top card. As he drew one from the deck, a loud popping noise erupted outside.

"Get down!" Aldrich dropped his cards on the coffee table and drew his gun in one smooth action.

"I've got the witness covered!" Laura yelled from the back of the house.

Dr. Devins and Luc hit the floor as a high-pitched whistling sound rent the air.

Luc hunkered behind the love seat, torn between not getting in the way of the marshals and wanting to crawl down the hallway to check on Priscilla. The last time he'd entrusted Priscilla's safety to someone, it hadn't turned out well. Just as he was about to make a dash for the hallway, another round of whistling exploded in the air.

A few feet away, Aldrich spoke into the microphone of his earpiece. "What's going on?"

The agent huddled to the left of the front door, peering out one of the side windows. Another round of pops startled Luc, making the muscles in his body jump. Through the curtains, the darkness outside brightened with more explosions.

"It's okay." Aldrich stood and holstered his gun. "The sheriff's department confirmed it's fireworks. The local high school is celebrating a big football win against their crosstown rivals. The game had been delayed, and it ended later than usual."

Luc scrambled to his feet. "You're sure it was just fireworks and not a diversion?"

"Yes," the agent said.

Luc's heart rate slowed and his breathing returned to normal, but the incident had given him an inkling of what Priscilla must have gone through for years. To think that every unexpected pop and bang could be a threat and every person who looked at you twice had to be considered as a potential threat until ruled otherwise would make anyone leery of others.

"Fireworks." Laura uncoiled herself from her position guarding Priscilla, who had been crammed into the far recesses of the bedroom's tiny closet. "It's been confirmed by the local sheriff's department." She holstered her weapon and stretched.

"Fireworks?" Priscilla emerged from the closet, staggering a little as the muscles in her left leg cramped in response to the stiff position she'd held for the past fifteen minutes.

Laura shot her an amused glance. "Unfortunately, no one from our team connected with the local sheriff's department to see if anything unusual was going on to-night. If we had, we'd have been alerted to the possibility of fireworks after the local high school football game."

Priscilla tried to focus her thoughts on the information being shared, but truth be told, she was just thankful it was only a fireworks show, which meant she—and Luc—was safe.

Laura yawned. "I need some coffee. You want some?"

Priscilla shook her head. "It will just wind me up more. I'm already jumpy."

"I hear you." Laura opened the bedroom door and stepped into the hallway, but didn't pull the door completely closed.

Priscilla sat on the edge of the bed, her limbs still shaky even though the danger had passed. Fireworks to celebrate a football team's victory—a normal, happy occasion. That was all. She breathed in and out slowly, counting to ten with each inhalation and exhalation.

As she focused on calming breaths, her mind flitted back to the conversation with Luc earlier, and she lost the rhythm of breathing. Her distress over the fight with Luc heightened as she recalled the snippy tone she'd used with him over discovering the dream was an actual memory.

Even as the angry words had poured out of her mouth, she couldn't deny there was a connection between them, one that had sprung up gossamer thin from the moment she'd met his gaze at the hair salon. Those vivid blue eyes had reached deep into her soul and touched her heart. She didn't believe in love at first sight—that old trope was trotted out only in fairy tales and romance movies.

Then why did her heart flutter when he was near?

That he felt something for her wasn't in doubt—she just wasn't sure what that was.

Her phone rang and she grabbed it, grateful for the distraction from her own thoughts. A quick check on caller ID revealed Mac was calling.

"Priscilla, are you sure you're okay?" Mac's calm voice on the other end of the phone soothed her frazzled nerves.

"I guess I'm still jittery after the fireworks scare." That was all Mac needed to know. If she were being honest, the anxiousness had more to do with remembering bits of her wedding to Luc.

"That's understandable. We shouldn't have been caught off guard about the school activities." Mac cleared his throat. "I didn't get a chance to talk with you privately before I had to head back earlier, but I wanted to talk about Dr. Devins."

"The shrink?" She paced the length of the bedroom.

"I think he'd rather be referred to as a psychiatrist. He has a specialty in hypnotherapy."

That halted her movements. "Wait—is this the doctor you mentioned a couple of months ago, who might be able to help me recover my memories of that night?"

"Yes, he's the one. We usually don't have civilians along on protection details. However, Dr. Devins has been trained by the marshals to accompany agents to safe houses to help interview witnesses who have memory issues."

"Like me." Priscilla resumed her pacing. "What's the plan?"

"For Dr. Devins to have a hypnosis session with you tomorrow morning."

"Okay." Maybe at last she'd remember more than the shooting.

"Priscilla?"

Something about his tone made the hairs on the back of her neck prickle. "What aren't you telling me?" She rubbed her forehead.

"It's something at the Grammar crime scene."

She frowned. "The witness Culvert killed."

"Yes." Mac didn't elaborate for several seconds, and the tension in her shoulders tightened. "This afternoon, when the techs returned to finish processing the scene, they discovered an envelope in the mailbox."

Priscilla was too wired to follow Mac's train of thought clearly. "If he just died, that wouldn't be unusual, right?"

Mac paused. "It wouldn't be if it hadn't been addressed to me."

She gripped the phone tighter, not sure she wanted to hear what the envelope contained. "What was in it?"

"A printout of your photo with the words *You're next* scrawled across it."

She nearly stopped breathing even as her heart rate galloped. "When…?" She tried again. "When was it taken?"

"I've already shared this with the team at the safe house. Everyone's on high alert. He will *not* get close enough to hurt you." Mac talked fast. "My supervisors agree that you'll be safer staying put with the extra security than moving you again."

She refused to be distracted from the question that burned in her mind. "What was I wearing in the photo, Mac?"

"Scrubs. You were wearing the scrubs from yesterday's trip to the clinic."

ELEVEN

Priscilla tied her sneakers, then yawned. The brightness of the morning sun streaming in through the venetian blinds did little to improve her mood. The revelation that Culvert had been close enough to her yesterday to snap a photo had her tossing and turning all night. That, and shame at the way she'd treated Luc last night.

The bottom line was that she didn't remember him, and she wasn't sure she could trust him. But that was no excuse for being mean. She didn't want to face him, didn't want to face anyone, but her stomach growled in protest of hiding out.

The aroma of coffee brewing greeted her as soon as she opened the door. *I can do this.* She glanced at her shaky hands, then rubbed them on the side of her jeans. A little jumpiness was normal for someone in her situation. The marshals would assume it had something to do with the photograph. No one would tie it to her kitchen encounter with Luc. Had anyone filled him in on the recent findings?

Myers stood with a mug in his left hand outside the kitchen. His head jerked and his right hand immediately went to his holster when she approached. Then he relaxed his stance. "Good morning, Priscilla."

"I see I'm not the only one on high alert." She paused in front of him. "Coffee?"

Myers moved out of the way to allow her to pass. In the kitchen, Aldrich fried bacon while Marshal Devins filled mugs with coffee.

"Oh, I need some of that." Priscilla stepped forward, then noticed Luc tucked into the far corner with his own mug in hand. Their eyes met, but she quickly dropped hers to focus on fixing her mug with one packet of sugar and a dollop of cream. "I'll get out of the way. Too many cooks and all that." With a smile of thanks, she scurried out of the kitchen and into the living room, where Dr. Devins sat with his feet propped on the coffee table.

"Good morning, Priscilla." He straightened. "How did you sleep?"

She settled into the club chair and wrapped her hands around the mug. "Not well, knowing Culvert won't stop until I'm dead." She lifted the mug and breathed in the scent before taking a tentative sip. Still too hot for her to drink.

"I can see how that would impact your sleep." Dr. Devins sipped his coffee. "How are you holding up?"

"I don't know." She sighed. "I feel like I'm dancing on a razor's edge, and one wrong move will send me sliding down."

"That's only natural, given the events of the past few days." He sat quietly for a few seconds. "The marshals will catch this guy."

"I know." *But it might be too late.*

"Did Mac tell you why I'm here?"

Priscilla nodded. "He mentioned you wanted to hypnotize me to bring back more memories."

"With Luc in the picture, I think there's more of a chance that you'll remember even more details about the shooting and recover the missing hours too." Dr. Devins regarded her over the rim of his cup. "I understand you've tried hypnosis before with no luck."

"That's right." She blew across the coffee surface in her mug to cool it down, then took a small sip. Perfect—nice and rich, just the way she liked it.

"When was that?"

"It was a year after I entered the program. My previous handler thought it could help make my testimony stronger, but I didn't remember anything new at all."

"Luc told me this morning that you remembered something on your own, which is a good sign that maybe your brain is ready to handle the other memories."

"He told you about the dream?" Priscilla put down her mug with a thunk. That had been a private memory, something she didn't want to share with anyone else.

Her voice must have been sharper than she realized because Dr. Devins held up a hand. "Whoa there. Don't shoot the messenger. Luc only said you had a brief memory. He didn't provide any specific details."

Priscilla offered a smile. "I have very little of my life that I don't have to share—with law enforcement—so I tend to be protective."

"I understand."

"Do you really think remembering more details is going to help us catch this killer?" She was willing to try almost anything to finally be free from the hiding and lying. The more details she could remember, the better chance the federal prosecutor had of putting Culvert in prison once the FBI captured him. But could hypnosis uncover memories that would help the investigation or only show her she had nothing left to remember? She wasn't sure which prospect scared her more.

Dr. Devins leaned forward, his expression earnest.

"I do. I think you're ready, probably more ready than you'll ever be. You just need a little push in the right direction. Are you game to try again?"

"Yes." She summoned a shaky smile. Now that more was at stake than just remembering additional details about the murders, she was willing to try again. "When?"

"After breakfast?"

As if on cue, Laura appeared in the doorway, a platter of crisp bacon in one hand and a bowl of scrambled eggs in the other. "Breakfast is served in the dining room."

Luc stared at his face in the mirror above the bathroom sink, willing his stomach to stop flip-flopping. The inner turmoil was turning his breakfast of bacon, eggs and toast into one soggy mess. The discovery he'd learned over breakfast regarding the threatening note delivered to a dead witness's house had put a damper on the conversation. Priscilla had been particularly quiet during the meal, whether because of the note, the events of the past forty-eight hours or the upcoming hypno-therapy session, Luc didn't know. All he did know was that he was nervous about the session and worried about her safety.

Dr. Devins had requested his attendance during the session with Priscilla because the psychiatrist believed Luc's presence would help shake loose her lost memories, given he had been with her during the pivotal time she needed to recall.

Luc splashed water on his face, then used the hand towel to blot his face dry. He must be calm or he'd rattle Priscilla. The last thing he wanted to do was drive all thoughts of the events leading up to and surrounding their wedding completely out of Priscilla's mind—forever. This session could lead to the resolution of their marriage, freeing them both. Why that prospect wasn't as attractive as it had been a few days ago, he didn't want to think about.

A rap on the door nearly made him drop the towel. He hung it back up and opened the door. Myers stood outside, his face impassive. "Dr. Devins is ready."

Luc followed Myers to the bedroom where the session would take place.

At the door, Myers turned. "We'll be right outside this door, and we've stepped up patrols around the house."

Luc nodded. The marshals had dressed in more casual clothes today, allowing their shoulder harnesses and holstered weapons to be on display. Luc hoped the show of force would help Priscilla relax enough for the hypnotherapy to work.

Myers stepped back as Luc opened the door. Priscilla sat on the bed, and Dr. Devins had dragged two of the dining room chairs into the room. The blinds had been closed to block out some of the morning sun.

"Luc, thank you for joining us. Priscilla, please lie against the pillows. Luc will sit in the chair beside you." Dr. Devins directed Luc to his position. "When I start the session, your job is to be quiet."

"Got it." Luc repositioned a chair closer to the bed. He tried not to think about how beautiful she looked.

Priscilla reclined on top of the blankets, her shoulders and head propped up with pillows.

"Good." Dr. Devins turned off the overhead light, leaving the room bathed in the light of a single bedside lamp. "Priscilla, would you be comfortable if Luc held your hand during the session? I often find that having physical contact with someone close, or, in your case, someone you're trying to remember, is helpful."

Luc looked down at Priscilla, who puckered her brow. For some reason, he hoped she'd say yes.

When she nodded, he didn't hesitate to reach for her left hand. No wedding ring. Neither one of them had had a ring when they tied the knot—that had been first on his to-do list the following day. He'd planned to purchase two inexpensive gold bands.

Now he lightly held her bare hand, reveling in the feel of her soft skin against his own palm. *Lord, let this hypnosis jog her memory about that night.* Her disconnected past bothered him more than he let on, but there were bigger issues at stake, such as Priscilla's need to recall more details about the shooting that could help federal agents recapture Culvert.

Priscilla hadn't looked at him for more than a few seconds since their argument last night. Today she'd been standoffish around him. He only hoped the memories of those missing hours—hours that included marrying him—would return full force.

Dr. Devins settled into the chair to Priscilla's right. "Ready?"

Priscilla nodded.

"Good. Now I want you to relax." Dr. Devins began taking Priscilla through some relaxation methods, instructing her to feel the tension draining from her body.

If Luc was any judge, it wasn't working. Priscilla's body stayed as rigid as a board. He imagined she was trying, but her inability to unwind was evidenced by her unyielding hand.

Dr. Devins leaned forward and touched her arm. "Priscilla."

Her eyes flew open. "Yes?"

"You're having a hard time relaxing." Dr. Devins didn't put it as a question to her. "Is it because you're afraid it won't work or that the hypnosis will reveal more than you would like? Those are two very common concerns."

She bit her lip, a gesture Luc had noted previously when she was fearful. "I didn't remember anything the first time I tried this. I want it to work but I can't seem to quiet my mind. Everything's all jumbled up inside." She removed her hand from Luc's and brushed her hair away from her forehead.

"Should I go?" Luc didn't want to leave, but if his being there meant she couldn't relax enough to give hypnosis a try, then he would.

"Do you want Luc to go?" Dr. Devins continued to address Priscilla in a gentle voice. "Are you concerned you might disappoint him if you don't remember meeting and marrying him?"

Priscilla scrunched up her nose. "I don't know. I suppose it's possible."

Luc knew just how she felt. He'd entered the hair salon to confront her about leaving him and to ask for an annulment. Learning that she'd witnessed a horrific shooting and had blanked out most of the hours surrounding the incident had put a new spin on the anger and hurt he'd wrestled with over the years.

He had never told anyone in his family about his marriage—how could he when he couldn't produce a bride?—but he had wanted to tell his grandparents, given his father's parents had had a whirlwind romance of their own. His own parents had had a short courtship as well.

What he hadn't explained to Priscilla was that they weren't complete strangers. As fifteen-year-olds, they, along with a dozen or so other teens and adults, had spent two weeks together as part of a summer mission trip to the Navajo Nation Reservation in Arizona. Helping to build a community center and playing soccer with the reservation kids had forged a bond between them. He had recognized her instantly when he saw her again at the Last Chance Casino, and she had remembered him as well. With everything that had happened over the past couple of days, Luc hadn't had time to discuss that mission trip with Priscilla.

That was why he'd not hesitated in asking Priscilla to marry him within hours of meeting her—he'd been sure it was the right response to her losing her job and being banned from the casino. With both parents deceased and no other family around and her rent due the next day, Priscilla was on the brink of becoming homeless and destitute. His own bank account had a healthier margin, and he was slated to start a new job in a week that would more than support himself and a wife. With hindsight, he ruefully acknowledged the idea of rescuing a pretty woman had appealed to his ego and played a larger part in his proposal than he originally admitted to himself.

But it was obvious Priscilla had no room in her life for a relationship, not when she was in witness protection. If only he could keep in mind that his intention in seeking her out was not to rekindle anything, but to extinguish their marriage to free them both.

Luc heaved himself off the chair. "I think I should go. Maybe you'll be able to relax better." Priscilla didn't try to stop him with either a word or a glance.

Dr. Devins clicked his pen. "That might be best."

Nothing for it but to leave. He walked to the door and opened it but couldn't resist one final glance back at Priscilla. To his chagrin, her focus was entirely on Dr. Devins, who spoke softly to her in words he couldn't hear. So much for needing his presence after all.

TWELVE

As the door clicked shut behind Luc, Priscilla's shoulders slumped. She had been acutely aware of him beside her, the warmth from his hand as he held hers. But her anxiousness from the past couple of days threatened to derail the doctor's trip down memory lane. Even though Luc had abided by the psychiatrist's instructions and remained quiet, she sensed Luc willing her to remember more of the past. That unsaid expectation had only added to her tenseness.

"Shall we start over?"

She nodded and closed her eyes again, sending a short prayer that this time she would successfully recall more of those missing hours.

"Breathe in and out to my count of ten," Dr. Devins instructed.

Priscilla concentrated on breathing in and out, listening to the cadence of Dr. Devins's voice as it rose and fell in a soothing rhythm. The room morphed into a noisy casino with the flashing lights from the slot machines bouncing off the mirrors that adorned the ceiling and walls. Priscilla wove her way expertly through the crowds, neatly avoiding customers with grabby hands.

She approached a high-top table meant for four people, but which instead seated seven young men. Their intoxicated behavior and raucous banter about one member getting ready to tie the knot informed her that this was a bachelor party. At least bachelor parties usually tipped well. With a plastered-on smile, she asked brightly, "What can I get you gentlemen?"

A brown-haired man in the party made a lewd comment that triggered guffaws from all the other members, except for one—a tall blond with piercing blue eyes, who stood a little back from the group. There was something familiar about him. He shot her an apologetic smile as she took the rest of their drink orders. When she got to the blond man, instead of ordering vodka shooters like his friends, he asked for club soda with a twist of lime and an order of nachos and chicken wings.

As if someone had hit the fast-forward button on a DVD, the scene shifted to later that same evening. In the darkened hallway leading to the employee break room, Priscilla grappled with the brown-haired man from the bachelor party.

The man pressed her against the wall and planted sloppy kisses on her face and neck while his hands groped her body. Her back pressed hard against the wall, giving her no room to maneuver away or counter his attack. She bucked her body against his to throw him off balance, but he merely grunted, then yanked her hair to position her head where he wanted it and continued his assault.

The man shifted and Priscilla jammed her high heel into the instep of his foot. He yelped and sprang back, anger replacing his desire.

She darted to the side, but his hand whipped out and grabbed her upper arm in a viselike grip. Priscilla cried out in pain, but suddenly, the pressure on her arm was gone. She turned to see the blond man absorb a blow to the face from her attacker before punching the other man, knocking her attacker to the floor. Her attacker's jaw sported an angry mark on his white skin while her rescuer had corresponding redness on his cheek.

The man on the floor massaged his jaw while glaring up at the blond man. Her attacker then focused on Priscilla. "I'll get you for this. Just wait and see." He stood and shouldered past, bumping her into the wall, as he stalked off.

"Are you okay?" Her rescuer handed her a handkerchief.

"Thanks for coming to my rescue." As she vigorously attempted to erase all marks the man had left on her face with his sloppy kisses, she tried to lighten the moment with a question. "Who carries handkerchiefs anymore?"

"I do. You never know when you'll need to offer one." He looked more closely at her flushed face. "Are you sure you're all right? Do you want to see a doctor?"

"No, I don't need a doctor." She blotted underneath her eyes to clean up any smudged mascara. Her hand trembled but she concentrated on erasing any signs of the attack. Gerald, the pit boss, would have a fit if she went on the floor looking anything less than a million bucks.

"Here, you missed some." Luc gently took the handkerchief from her hand and wiped something off her right cheek. He leaned closer as if to inspect the area, his body in front of hers.

She sucked in a breath to calm her nerves. "You look very familiar. Do we know each other?"

"My name's Luc."

Then it clicked. "Luc Langsdale?"

He nodded. "Priscilla Makin, right?"

It was her turn to nod. "I can't believe it's really you. How long has it been since that summer on the reservation?"

"I think about seven or eight years."

"What's going on, Priscilla!"

Priscilla jumped at the sound of Gerald's booming voice.

The smaller, weasel-looking man stood at the end of the hallway, his ever-present clipboard tucked under one armpit. "I've just received very disturbing news from a Mr. Todd Smith, who claims you lured him back here and pretended you were interested in some hanky-panky."

Priscilla couldn't believe it. How dare that scumbag pin this on her. "What? I didn't lure anyone anywhere. That man hurt me."

Gerald raised an eyebrow. She cringed. Her boss always took the side of the customer, especially ones who threw around money. Not long after she started working at the Last Chance, she had stopped reporting customers who made her uncomfortable with their inappropriate comments after Gerald refused to listen.

"That's the last time you insult a customer." Gerald pointed his finger at her. "You're fired."

"Priscilla, it's time to wake up." Dr. Devins spoke softly, jerking her out of the memories.

Breathing hard, Priscilla opened her eyes, her heart pounding as the memories continued to pour through her mind.

"It's okay. Take a few deep breaths."

She obeyed, her racing pulse slowing down.

"What do you remember?" Dr. Devins asked in a calm voice.

Priscilla told him, the words spilling over themselves

as she raced to get everything out in case the memories faded back into the recesses of her mind. "Gerald threw me out of the casino and wouldn't even let me collect my things."

"About what time would you say that happened?"

"Time?" Priscilla gripped her fingers tightly together. "Maybe near midnight? I think it happened close to the end of my shift." She loosened her hands. "The casinos don't have clocks and we're not allowed to wear watches or carry cell phones while on the floor. The pit boss would tell us to take breaks and go off the clock. Management wanted its staff to honestly say we don't know the time if a guest asked. Maybe Luc would know for sure."

"We'll ask him." Dr. Devins jotted something down on the yellow notepad on his lap. "When did you run into Luc again that evening?"

"I don't know." She pushed her hair out of her eyes. "That's it. My mind's back to being a blank page up until the shooting."

"Don't worry—that's a great start. It's likely that once you've started remembering, other scenes from that evening will become clearer to you."

"You mean like this might have broken a logjam? That soon I'll be able to remember everything from that night?"

"It's highly likely the other memories will shake loose on their own now that you've started remembering."

"You don't know how much I've longed to remember more than the few bits and pieces I've already shared with the marshals." She lay back against the pillows as a wave of tiredness crashed over her.

He patted her hand. "I understand. Just remember not to push things."

"I won't." She stifled a yawn.

"We'll try another session after lunch." Dr. Devins stood. "You should rest now." He turned out the lamp and left the room, closing the door with a soft click.

Priscilla tugged the top quilt over her body and snuggled down as her eyelids drooped shut. At least she'd remembered meeting Luc and their shared past on the mission trip as teenagers. Maybe later today she'd actually recall marrying him.

Luc sliced onions, then dumped them into the sizzling skillet along with the heated olive oil. Cooking relaxed him, and he needed something to do while Priscilla rested after her hypnosis session. Dr. Devins had come out forty minutes ago with news that the session had gone well, but he wouldn't share any details.

"Smells good." Aldrich sniffed appreciatively as he entered the kitchen. "What's cooking?"

"Philly cheesesteaks." Luc added red and green pepper slices to the onions, then stirred the veggies in the pan.

"Impressive." Aldrich uncapped a water bottle. "I usually just grab a PB&J for lunch."

Luc opened a package of sub rolls. "Why go with what's easy when you can whip up something a little more filling and tasty?"

"Said like a man who takes food much more seriously than I do."

Luc separated the tops from the bottoms of the sub rolls and lined them up on a cookie sheet.

Aldrich leaned against the counter. His poise appeared relaxed to any observer but Luc sensed a coiled readiness in the other man. The recent photo of Priscilla had put everyone on edge.

"How come you married Priscilla?"

To buy himself time while considering how to answer, Luc pushed the onions and peppers around in the pan, then lowered the heat. He slid the rolls into the wall oven.

Aldrich took another swig from his water bottle. "Avoiding the question?"

"Maybe." Luc flipped the flank steak, which was browning nicely under the heat of the broiler.

"Hey, man, if you don't want to tell me, that's okay." Aldrich watched him separate provolone cheese slices. "It's too bad that she doesn't remember you at all."

"You're telling me. She had a good session with Dr. Devins, but even though he didn't tell me what she said, I'm hoping she'll recall our meeting soon."

A doorbell chime sounded and Aldrich pulled his phone out of his pocket. "A text I need to address. Call me when lunch is ready—and thanks. It will sure beat PB&J."

"Will do." Luc sliced the meat. *Please, Lord, let Priscilla have recalled something helpful. And help the marshals catch whoever is trying to harm her.*

Pulling the rolls from the oven, he assembled the sandwiches, then wrapped them in foil before returning them to the oven to warm and melt the cheese under a low temperature.

As he cleaned up the kitchen, his mind returned to washing dishes last night with Priscilla before he'd spoiled it with his idiotic comment about being married. At least things had calmed down since they'd arrived. Maybe they'd catch Culvert soon, and he and Priscilla could finally have a real conversation about what had happened between them in Vegas.

He rinsed the last pan and put it in the dish drainer.

A movement outside the window over the kitchen sink caught his eye. Someone was out there, but then again, someone was supposed to be out there—a pair of marshals patrolling the perimeter.

There it was again, a flash of light like a reflection off a mirror. What if it wasn't the marshals? What if it was—

The glass shattered and Luc dropped to the floor.

THIRTEEN

Someone shook Priscilla's shoulder and she blinked, trying to banish the vestiges of sleep from her mind.

"We have to leave. Now!" The urgency in Laura's voice penetrated the fog of sleep, jolting Priscilla fully awake.

"What's happened?" Priscilla scrambled to find her shoes. The marshal stood to the side of the room's single window and peered through a slit in the blinds with her gun drawn. "Will you please tell me what's going on?"

"Someone took a shot at Luc through the kitchen window." Laura faced the window as she spoke. "He's okay, but we're leaving."

Priscilla's fingers shook as she tied her laces. "Ready."

"Good." Laura moved away from the window and spoke into her earpiece. "I'm leaving with the witness."

Priscilla hugged herself to stop the trembling that had taken over. When would this nightmare end? They should have left last night, but Mac assured her the photo of her in scrubs was snapped leaving the clinic, not entering this safe house.

"Let's go." Laura motioned for Priscilla to come up behind her as the marshal eased open the door.

Myers and Aldrich stood directly outside the room with their guns drawn. Myers nodded toward Aldrich. "Priscilla, you'll go with Aldrich. Devins will cover the rear and I'll be the front man."

Priscilla bit back asking about Luc. The marshals didn't need to be distracted from doing their job.

Aldrich drew Priscilla closer as Myers moved down the hallway toward the other back bedroom.

"Witness headed to rendezvous one." Myers spoke into his earpiece.

Aldrich kept his hand on Priscilla's shoulder, his body shielding hers. Adrenaline coursed through her entire being. Her blood pounded in her ears.

Myers opened the bedroom's door and entered. "Clear."

Aldrich and Priscilla followed, Laura taking up residence at the doorway, her gun trained down the hallway. Myers pressed his hand to his ear, then nodded. "Copy that." He turned to Aldrich. "Luc and Dr. Devins are in position, ready for the diversion."

Diversion? That didn't sound like a good idea, not when somebody was trying to kill her. She opened her mouth to ask, but Myers spoke first from his position underneath an open window. "On my count, I'll go through first and you'll follow."

Myers counted softly. "One, two, three."

An explosion shook the house, the sound much louder and harsher than last night's fireworks. Priscilla crouched, but Aldrich urged her up, tugging her toward the open window. Myers had his torso through. Then he disappeared from view.

"Your turn." Aldrich lifted her through the opening to Myers, who grabbed her around the waist. Once free of the window, Priscilla dropped to the ground behind the cover of several tall boxwoods. She crawled to the right as Aldrich came through, followed quickly by Laura. They remained crouched behind the shrubbery.

Two SUVs facing the street were parked side by side in the gravel driveway. "Package is ready." Myers half rose from his crouch, gun raised. "Let's move."

Aldrich resumed his position as bodyguard and rested his hand on her shoulder. "Everything's going to be okay."

Myers sprinted toward the nearest SUV, rounding the front of the vehicle to access the driver's door. He signaled them to follow.

Aldrich applied pressure on Priscilla's shoulder. "On the count of three, we'll make a run for the first vehicle. Get in through the back door and move to the far side of the passenger seat."

She nodded, then slightly straightened as he counted. When he reached three, she sprang to her feet, Aldrich beside her, and they ran pell-mell to the SUV. Aldrich wrenched open the back door and she leaped in, sliding across the bench seat. Aldrich slammed the door behind him as the passenger-side door opened to admit Laura.

Myers threw the car in gear and hit the accelerator just as Laura shut the door. The second SUV peeled out after them.

Aldrich holstered his firearm, then punched in a number on his cell. "Mac? It's Aldrich. You're on speakerphone."

"Didn't Myers tell you I'm about twenty minutes away? What? You couldn't wait?" Mac's voice held an amused tenor.

"Someone took a shot at Luc through the kitchen window. Luckily, the shooter missed his target. We're all in the SUVs heading west." Aldrich paused. "All but

Peters. He was found shot in the forehead at close range in the woods behind the house."

Mac uttered a soft curse.

"Thompson found his body about thirty seconds before the shot was fired into the house." Aldrich shifted in his seat. "The shooter took Peters's weapon and cell phone."

Priscilla blinked back tears. She hadn't met Peters, only heard his name as one of the marshals on patrol outside. Now he was dead because of her.

"Walk me through it all." Mac's voice had a hard edge to it.

Priscilla leaned her head back as Aldrich, with input from Laura and Myers, recounted what had happened. Priscilla's body relaxed when she heard Luc was in the second SUV with Marshal Thompson and Dr. Devins. She turned her head to stare blindly out the window at trees, now nearly barren of leaves.

Aldrich touched her arm. "You okay?"

"I guess so." She gave him a tired smile. "How did he find me?"

The marshal frowned. "We took evasive actions to avoid being followed. We don't have any answers yet. The FBI will collect any evidence the intruder left behind at the safe house."

Priscilla drew in a ragged breath. "Did Peters have a family?"

Aldrich nodded. "A wife, who's expecting their first baby in a few months."

A tear slid down her cheek, and she made no attempt to brush it off. "I'm so sorry. This is all because of me."

"Listen to me. Peters knew what he signed up for. We all did. It's a dangerous job. We're fully aware that we might not make it home one day." He looked her straight in the eye. "This is not your fault. It's Culvert who's to blame, not you."

She tucked a strand of hair behind her ear, thoughts churning inside her brain like towels tumbling in a dryer. "I don't get the timing."

"What do you mean?"

"Culvert had more than five years to track down and eliminate me, but I've had a rather quiet existence in WITSEC up until three days ago."

Aldrich rubbed his jaw. "Why now?"

Luc ripped open a packet of ketchup and squeezed it onto the paper wrapper. The marshals had reconvened at a Sleepy Time Residence Inn, commandeering two rooms with connecting doors. Each unit had two bedrooms and a kitchenette. Based on the length of time driving and their westerly direction, Luc guessed they were close to the West Virginia–Kentucky border. Right after their arrival, Devins and Aldrich had disappeared, returning to the inn with sacks from a fast-food burger chain.

The marshals then directed Priscilla and Luc to eat at the tiny kitchen table, while they took over the small living room for a private conference. Which was fine by Luc, as he'd welcomed some time alone with Priscilla.

Luc took a sip of his iced tea. "How are you holding up?"

"I wish people would stop asking me that." She unwrapped a straw and pushed it into the top of her Diet Coke.

"Sorry." He dunked a french fry into the ketchup before eating it.

She raised her eyebrows. "Come on. Out with it."

"What do you mean?"

She sighed. "What you've been dying to ask me, of course."

He chuckled. "Am I that transparent?"

Priscilla traced a line of condensation along the side of her plastic cup. "The good news is that I did remember meeting you and spending time with you while on the mission trip when we were teenagers." She related the events up until her boss fired her.

He bit back his frustration at the brick wall her memories had come up against. At least he wasn't a total stranger to her any longer—that was progress.

She hesitated. "Would you say a blessing for our lunch?"

Surprised, but pleased, he nodded, then offered a short prayer of thanksgiving for their safety and a petition to catch Culvert soon. They ate in silence for a few minutes.

Priscilla chewed a french fry and swallowed. "I've been thinking about that night. My memory is like one of those old reel-to-reel films that's being restored. Sometimes the frames are out of order, but sometimes there are several frames intact together."

"You'll get there." Luc finished his burger. "You'd tried hypnotherapy when you first entered the program, right?"

"Yeah, that didn't turn out so hot. Dr. Devins is better. The other doctor blamed me for not remembering. He said I was intentionally repressing the memories. I never went back to him."

Luc wiped his mouth with a paper napkin. "When did Mac mention it again?"

"I think it was maybe ten weeks ago, when we were going over my initial witness statement to prepare for the trial. He asked if I would be willing to undergo hypnosis again."

"And you said yes without any hesitation?" He popped the last bit of burger into his mouth.

"I agreed, as long as it wasn't with the previous doctor. Mac assured me that they'd lined up a new psychologist. Dr. Devins has done more research into hypnotherapy and published a few papers in medical journals. Earlier, Dr. Devins said we could do another session this afternoon, but I guess that will have to wait until we're settled in a new location."

Luc wasn't sure there was such a place. "Who else would know you were considering hypnosis again?"

Priscilla narrowed her eyes and her body stiffened. "You don't think it's a coincidence that someone is trying to kill me now that I've resumed hypnotherapy?"

"No, I don't." Luc kept his voice low, his eyes never leaving her pale face. "I think someone doesn't want you to recall any more details about what happened that night."

FOURTEEN

Luc snagged a couple of paper towels, then grabbed the bag of microwave popcorn. After their meal, several more marshals had arrived bearing groceries, fresh clothes and serious expressions. Based on their somber looks, Luc didn't waste any time suggesting to Priscilla that she join him in one of the bedrooms for a movie on TV. The last thing she needed was to overhear the marshals debriefing about the morning's harrowing events.

"Did you find something to watch?" He couldn't help but smile seeing Priscilla in a pair of flannel pajama bottoms and a faded University of Virginia sweatshirt, her damp hair loosely braided after her shower. It did his heart good to see her relaxing. He could see vestiges of the carefree teenager he'd met that long-ago summer in the Arizona desert.

"There's not much on at five on a Wednesday, mostly home improvement shows or the news."

Luc joined Priscilla on the small love seat squeezed into one corner of the bedroom. He plumped a pillow behind his back and head, then handed her a paper towel. "Choose whatever you'd like to watch. To be honest, I'm just enjoying the quiet time with you."

She waggled the remote at him. "I need something

to take my mind off everything that's happened." She cracked a smile, the first he'd seen in a long time. "We could watch Turner Classic Movies. I love to watch old black-and-white films, and Turner is playing *Suspicion* with Cary Grant and Joan Fontaine."

Luc returned her smile. "I've been meaning to watch that one. Hitchcock, right?" He held out the bag of popcorn to Priscilla.

She popped a handful of kernels in her mouth and nodded. "*Suspicion* it is." She leaned back and snuggled down a bit, her body slumping sideways just enough for their shoulders to touch.

When she didn't move away, Luc relaxed too. This was normal, like any other couple watching a movie. Except that they weren't a couple at all.

Watching the film close to her distracted him in a whole other way. He breathed in the flowery scent of her shampoo, the fragrance reminding him of the small bouquet of flowers she'd carried at their wedding.

As he reached into the popcorn bag, his hand brushed hers. Against his better judgment, he ate more popcorn than he really wanted just to have more opportunities to "accidentally" touch her hand. All too soon, the bag was empty, and Luc placed it on the end table.

At the climactic scene where Grant's character drives recklessly on a narrow road along a cliff, Luc glanced at Priscilla. Her eyes were closed and her breathing even. His attention shifted from the TV to his sleeping companion. He shifted slightly, raised his right arm, and her head lolled onto his shoulder, fitting snugly against him. Memories of their brief time together in Vegas threatened to overwhelm his senses.

She sighed in her sleep, and he laid a featherlight kiss on the top of her head. The rest of the movie played out, but his attention was solely on Priscilla. His eyes traced the contours of her face, noting the faint worry line creasing her forehead. He gently traced a path from her hairline to her jawline with his index finger. Beneath the pad of his finger, her skin was soft.

Priscilla stirred and opened her eyes, sleep darkening the blue of her irises. His hand stilled at her jaw. When she didn't shove it away, he continued his exploration, moving his fingers across her brow and lightly outlining her eyebrows.

"I'd forgotten how beautiful you are." His whisper stirred a wisp of hair onto her cheek, and he tucked the strand behind her ear.

"I didn't know you existed until three days ago." Her voice, low and husky from her short nap, inflamed his heart. "Everything's mixed up inside my head."

"Shhh." He pressed his index finger lightly across her mouth. "It's okay. Everything's a bit mixed up in mine too."

Her lips tensed against his finger. Was that a kiss? His hopefulness awakened a fresh desire to cover her mouth with his own, but he should quash that yearning. He hadn't searched for Priscilla to start a relationship.

Removing his finger, he waited, his eyes searching hers for a signal as to what she wanted. What he saw in their welcoming depths made him want to close the gap between them. But he didn't move a muscle, willing to let her make the first move.

"Luc?" The question hung in the air.

"Yes?" His gaze dropped to her mouth, and he could almost taste the saltiness from the popcorn that must coat her lips.

When her tongue darted out to her bottom lip, he pulled back slightly, needing to put space between them.

His resolve had been weakened to the point that any second he might break the promise just made to himself.

"Would you kiss me?"

Her request made him smile. "With pleasure."

Slowly, Luc fanned his hand across her cheek. He ran his fingers through the silkiness of her braid. Her eyes darkened, and her own hand reached up to touch his face, stroking her fingers along his five o'clock shadow.

Priscilla tugged his head down and placed her lips on his mouth. Luc kissed her gently, wishing he could prolong the moment, but forcing himself to extract himself from her embrace.

Luc pushed himself up off the love seat, noting with a twinge of satisfaction that her own breathing had quickened.

"I'll go check on dinner plans." He grabbed up the empty popcorn bag and headed out the door. His senses reeled from the kiss that had reminded him with the force of a hurricane why he'd married this intriguing woman at the drop of a hat. He had wanted to give Priscilla his protection until she got back on her feet after losing her job. Memories of their time together as teens had made it easy to propose. When she'd left without a trace hours after their wedding, he had been more hurt than relieved. Learning why she had vanished had stirred compassion in his heart for his missing bride.

Lord, keep Priscilla safe and help me to stick to my plan to release both of us from our impetuous decision to marry.

On the couch Priscilla wrapped her hands around a cup of steaming coffee, breathing in the rich aroma of Starbucks' holiday blend. She hadn't had a chance to talk much with Luc over dinner last night, and had barely said hello to him this morning, making her self-conscious and more than a little awkward. What would he say to her? What should she say to him after begging him to kiss her?

Her eyes went to Luc standing at the kitchen counter. He stirred cream into his mug with a spoon, making lazy circles around the inside rim of the cup.

The movement brought immediately to mind his gentle touch last night. She ducked her head as heat stole up her cheeks in memory of his kiss. Truth be told, she hadn't been asleep the entire time. She had awakened but kept her eyes closed, enjoying the sensation of his fingertips gliding over the contours of her face. A warmth had invaded her, filling her with a mixture of tranquility and excitement. When she had opened her eyes and seen him staring at her, it had seemed natural to kiss him.

Last night, Laura had slept in the same room with Priscilla for security reasons, putting an end to any more kissing. Not that Priscilla had much experience with kissing. She'd had to keep the few men who had expressed interest in her at arm's length because delving deeper into a relationship didn't feel safe to her. Being in WITSEC meant she'd gotten used to relating on the surface level. Her head told her to keep her distance from Luc until she knew she would even have a life beyond witness protection. But that kiss had her doubting the wisdom of that idea.

"How'd you sleep?" Luc asked, breaking the silence between them. He sat down beside her, propping his sock feet up on the coffee table.

His body language helped to put her at ease, and some of her anxiety about the kiss melted away when he turned his warm gaze on her. "I slept okay." She lowered her voice. "Despite Laura's snoring."

Luc laughed. "I see I got the better end of the deal. Myers had no such unwelcome habits. I slept like a baby."

His cheerful admission irked her. Had she been the only one awake half the night thinking about their kiss? This was why she should stay far away from any hint of romantic entanglements—she would only make a fool of herself. She focused her attention on her coffee.

He moved closer and leaned in, his lips next to her ear. "Don't you know that babies wake up frequently during the night?" He winked, then straightened.

His admission made her laugh, relief easing the tension that had been building in her shoulders. "It wasn't as peaceful a night's rest as you would have me believe."

He sipped his coffee. "Not in the least. Are you surprised?"

Before she could respond, Aldrich arrived with bagels and cream cheese. Myers dragged the kitchen chairs to a small sitting area, and the three agents and Dr. Devins joined Luc and Priscilla for an impromptu breakfast.

Smearing cream cheese on an everything bagel, Myers took the lead. "Mac wanted us to go over the timeline again. We're overlooking something."

Luc selected a jalapeño bagel. "Like how Culvert knows exactly where to find Priscilla. That's bugged me all along."

"You found her." Aldrich took a bite out of his bagel.

"Yes, but it took me several years and a lot of digging," Luc said.

"Walk us through how you did it," Laura requested.

Priscilla munched on a blueberry bagel slathered with strawberry cream cheese as Luc relayed the twists and turns of hunting for her. Since she had heard his story already, she focused on the timelines. Prior to his capture, Culvert had had years to find her and kill her. Granted, Culvert might not have been aware of her as a witness until his defense attorney received notification of her existence during the discovery period. But even then, her identity had remained cloaked for security.

She licked a bit of cream cheese off her finger and took another bite. Culvert also had years to kill Grammar, who eschewed protection. Culvert's trial was scheduled for December 13, only weeks away now. That could be the impetus for his targeting witnesses.

But Culvert had been incarcerated for eighteen months without any escape attempts. His appendicitis hadn't been faked—it was a true emergency situation. Maybe Culvert had acted because the opportunity presented itself when he was hospitalized. But why not simply disappear? A man with his resources certainly had enough shady contacts to leave the country with falsified papers.

Then there were the attempts on her life. From all she'd heard—and seen—Culvert meticulously planned his assassinations. It was one of his hallmarks and the reason for his long, successful career. In contrast, the attempts on her life were amateurish in execution.

The niggling feeling that if Culvert wanted her dead, she would be dead, wouldn't go away.

Her focus shifted to dredging up all her memories of the Las Vegas shooting. Culvert had remained calm throughout the entire event, even picking up the shell casings with gloved hands on his way out. While she had been anything but calm—her body shaking in its hiding place under a room-service cart's thick skirting— Culvert moved stealthily through the room, making certain to leave nothing behind that would incriminate him.

She closed her eyes, her half-eaten bagel resting on a napkin in her lap. She'd stayed put for several long minutes after the kitchen door swung shut following Culvert's departure. Just when she started to part the heavy fabric to escape, the door opened. A tall man with dark hair wearing a navy blue suit entered, his outline hazy as if she viewed his form through a film.

Then the image vanished.

FIFTEEN

"Priscilla?" Myers's voice brought Priscilla back to the present.

"Yes?" Her cheeks warmed at being caught not paying attention to the discussion. "I'm sorry. I was woolgathering, as my grandmother used to say."

"I was saying that we need to go over the turn of events since the shooting three days ago. Let's review it step by step." Myers stood, brushing crumbs off his lap. "How about some fresh coffee to fuel our meeting? I know I could use another cup."

Priscilla looked down at her half cup of coffee. "I'm good." She didn't want to finish her bagel, and stuffed it into the paper sack along with the used napkins and empty individual cream cheese containers.

The others agreed that more coffee would be welcomed. Myers stepped into the kitchen to brew more java.

"Hey, are you okay?" Luc touched her hand briefly as Aldrich gathered the remains of their breakfast and Laura checked her phone for messages.

"I think so." She blew out a breath, not yet wanting to share her new memory of another man. It was probably her overactive imagination. Until she recalled the man more clearly, she would keep that "sighting" to herself. "I want to do something besides rehash everything. I hate feeling like a sitting duck, waiting for things to happen to me like some heroine of a fairy tale who reacts instead of acts."

"What would you do?" Luc's blue eyes were alight with interest.

"I'd start with motive." Priscilla sipped her tepid coffee.

"Not to point out the obvious, but surely Culvert's motive is that you'll testify against him. Your testimony alone could put him behind bars for the rest of his life."

She waved a hand at him. "I know that's what the marshals think, but I keep circling back to why now. Like you pointed out, Culvert's had years to track me down. But the thing is, I don't think he even knew I existed until the grand jury indictment. I'm just listed as Witness Number Thirty."

"I found you." Luc sounded smug.

"Yeah, but it took you several years—and you had access to government databases." Before she could explore her line of thought more, the marshals rejoined them in the living room, while Dr. Devins said he needed to return some phone calls and disappeared into one of the bedrooms.

Aldrich pulled out his notebook and read off the timeline. The map of events unfolded as everyone compared notes.

"When did Culvert kill Grammar?" Luc interjected.

Laura tapped her tablet. "It was the day of the fire at the safe house."

Priscilla set her coffee cup on the table. "Could Culvert have killed Grammar and set the fire?"

"Let me check the distance." Myers pulled up Google Maps on his phone to trace the route between Grammar's house in Roanoke, Virginia, and the safe house

near Petersburg, West Virginia. "It's about a three-and-
a-half-hour drive from Roanoke to the safe house. The
medical examiner hasn't narrowed down an exact time
of death, but puts it between 11:00 p.m. Monday and
4:00 a.m. Tuesday."

"Which means Culvert could have had time to kill
Grammar, then slip over to the safe house and set the fire
after midnight." Priscilla played a staccato rhythm on
the tabletop with her fingers as her thoughts raced from
one possibility to another. "That would also explain how
he was able to take that photo of me leaving the clinic."

Myers looked up from his phone. "We're exploring
the possibilities that there's an accomplice. We think
someone at the hospital where Culvert had his appendix removed helped to facilitate his escape."

Luc frowned. "How come this is the first time we're
hearing about a potential accomplice?"

Laura leveled a gaze at him. "Because you're not officially part of this investigation." She turned her attention
to Priscilla. "And she's a witness, therefore information
is on a need-to-know basis."

"And I didn't need to know this." Priscilla clasped her
hands together to stop her fidgeting. Her restlessness had
little to do with the caffeine boost and more to do with
an unsettled mind. It was as if they were spinning their
wheels and getting nowhere. Maybe another session with
Dr. Devins would shake loose more concrete facts that
would spur the marshals in a new direction, rather than
covering the same ground over and over again.

Myers continued, "Culvert corresponded with a
woman named Rachel Whitehurst while in jail. She
apparently imagined herself in love with Culvert." He
shook his head. "The way these women throw themselves at bad guys like Culvert will never cease to amaze

me. They know these men have done terrible things—in Culvert's case, he's been an alleged hired assassin for more than twenty years with hundreds of kills to his credit—but still they want to be with them."

Priscilla couldn't imagine wanting to talk with a man like Culvert, much less fall in love with him. She suppressed a shudder. "You think this Rachel might know where Culvert is?"

"If we can find her," Aldrich said. "She worked in Billing at the hospital where Culvert had his operation, and she hasn't been seen since his escape."

"How did this slip by until now?" Luc sounded as angry as Priscilla felt.

Myers visibly bristled, sitting up straighter in his chair. "Listen, the FBI followed protocol and worked with the sheriff's department on transporting Culvert to the hospital from the county jail. They even isolated him under an assumed name at the end of a hallway that didn't have access to the stairs or an elevator. He was handcuffed to the bed and had two deputies guarding him at all times. They did everything they could in the small window of time we had to make arrangements."

"But surely the FBI was aware that his so-called girlfriend worked at the hospital?" Priscilla tried to keep her voice even. The marshals worked hard to keep witnesses like herself safe from harm—it was a tough job mostly done behind the scenes. But she couldn't help but wonder who had dropped the ball with Culvert's security.

Aldrich sighed. "It was in Culvert's paperwork, but no one thought to look until after his escape."

"How exactly did he manage that?" Luc questioned.

"That's where we think Rachel helped him. Several hours before Culvert's escape, security footage shows her having a brief conversation with Deputy Calvin

Horner in the hospital parking lot just before Horner's overnight guard shift." Myers tapped his cell phone on his leg. "We think she must have passed along instructions or payment to Horner. A few hours into Horner's shift, one of the orderlies brought up two cups of coffee from the cafeteria, an arrangement Horner had made before coming to Culvert's floor. Security footage shows Horner bringing the cups into Culvert's room."

"But I thought both deputies had been drugged?" Priscilla frowned, as she recalled the details Mac had given her about Culvert's escape.

"They were. We think Horner slipped sedatives into both cups, making sure he was close enough to Culvert's bed that the prisoner could get the handcuff keys once the men were out."

"Didn't the nurses think something was off without the guard outside Culvert's room?" Priscilla still couldn't believe Culvert had escaped so easily.

Myers shook his head. "Horner timed the coffee delivery perfectly. Only four nurses were on the nighttime staff for that floor. It's usually five, but one had called out sick." He held up a hand as if to forestall their next question. "And before you ask, the FBI verified that the nurse had a legitimate reason." A small smile crossed his lips. "She was in Labor and Delivery two floors up having a baby, which no one could have foreseen."

"Unfortunately, we've not been able to question Horner because he had some sort of reaction to the sedative and has been in a coma." Aldrich sipped his coffee. "But the other deputy appears clean."

Priscilla organized her thoughts before speaking. "Horner laces the coffee with some sort of quick-acting sedative, gives one to the other deputy. They both drink it and pass out. Then what? That still doesn't explain how Culvert made it out of the hospital."

"He overpowered one of the nurses when she came into his room during her rounds, stuffed her in a closet and walked out wearing stolen scrubs, a surgical mask and hair cap. No one thought to check his ID—he'd used the nurse's ID to exit the secured floor during the middle of the night."

Priscilla touched the place where the small scar resided underneath the waistband of her jeans, remembering the pain and soreness that had lasted for days after her own emergency surgery. "I had my appendix out a few years ago, and it was tough to even sit up a few hours after surgery. How did he manage to walk out with no one noticing he'd just had surgery?"

"Maybe he's used to pain." Laura consulted her tablet, then continued. "Or maybe he had the ability to push it down until he could deal with it later. The hospital noted that some morphine went missing after Culvert's escape, along with extra bandages and dressings to take care of the wound site. It's possible that Rachel somehow got together those items for him. The FBI's still investigating that."

Myers's cell phone played the opening chords of Beethoven's Ninth Symphony, and he responded quickly to the call. "Hello?" The agent's demeanor changed as his body stiffened. The marshal listened, spoke a few muffled words, then disconnected the call.

Priscilla held her breath as Myers related the call's content.

"That was Mac. They have a lead on Rachel's whereabouts." Myers cracked a smile. "She finally used her cell phone, allowing our tech guys to ping her location. Get this—she's fifteen miles from here at a Motel 6 along Highway 32."

* * *

Two hours ago, three additional US marshals had shown up to guard Priscilla; and Myers, Aldrich and Laura had left to meet FBI agents and the local sheriff's department at the motel where Rachel Whitehurst might be. Dr. Devins and Priscilla decided to use the downtime for another hypnotherapy session in one of the bedrooms, while one marshal stayed outside and the other two worked their phones in the second bedroom with the door ajar.

Which left Luc with little to do. He folded the newspaper he'd read through twice and tossed it into the kitchen trash can. Nothing caught his attention on television. Without his phone, he tried to find something other than Christmas music on the clock radio, but gave up after hearing "Rockin' Around the Christmas Tree" on three separate channels. He surged to his feet to pace the few steps to the tiny kitchenette.

"Walls starting to close in on you?" Priscilla stood in the doorway.

"Yeah, you could say that." He noted the dark circles underneath her eyes. The stress must be playing havoc with her ability to sleep at night. He certainly hadn't been able to sleep soundly since he'd entered the hair salon three days ago. "How did it go with Dr. Devins this morning?"

Dropping into a chair at the small kitchen table, she rubbed her forehead. "I only remembered more details about the events surrounding the actual shooting."

Luc filled in what she left unsaid: *I didn't remember anything more about you.* It would certainly make it easier to officially put an end to their marriage if she couldn't recall their wedding. The thought filled him with disappointment more than the relief he'd expected. Shifting the topic away from her session, he asked, "Would you like something to drink?"

"Some water would be great." Priscilla hid a yawn behind her hand.

Dr. Devins came out of the bedroom, a small recorder in his hand, to join them at the table. "Priscilla? I think it might be helpful for you to hear what you said while under hypnosis. It might help to clarify the events of that night."

Luc handed Priscilla a bottle of water. "Should I leave?"

Priscilla looked at Dr. Devins. "I'd like Luc to stay, if that's okay."

"I don't think that would be a problem." Dr. Devins grabbed a water bottle out of the fridge. "Let me get the marshals."

Luc sat beside her at the table, while Dr. Devins spoke with the two marshals, who came out and joined them around the periphery of the table. Luc couldn't remember their names, having met many new faces over the past three days. The taller agent appeared to be a few years away from retirement, with his shock of gray hair and the crinkles around his eyes. The younger man had a smooth complexion that made guessing his age difficult.

The two marshals, both balancing notebooks and pens, nodded at Luc and Priscilla. Then the doctor hit the play button, filling the space with the sound of his voice as he softly counted down to pull Priscilla under hypnosis.

"What do you see?"

"The casino's kitchen."

"Why are you there?"

"I need to clean out my work locker. I didn't get a chance to do it earlier because Gerald had security escort me out of the casino." Priscilla's voice sounded tired.

This couldn't be easy for Priscilla to experience all over again. Luc wanted to cover her clenched hands with his own as they listened to her recollection, but her stiff posture made him decide not to follow through.

"Are the lockers near the kitchen?" Dr. Devins's questions gently pulled the narrative of that night from Priscilla's memories.

"Not exactly. I want to avoid being seen by my former boss, Gerald. I take a shortcut through the catering kitchen. It's closed for the night and right across from the staff locker room."

"Are you at your locker now?"

"Yes, the coast is clear. I grab my extra clothes and personal items, and stuff them into the reusable shopping bag I keep in my locker." The tenor of Priscilla's voice changed slightly, taking on a note of anxiety.

"What's happening now?"

"As I'm leaving the locker room, I hear voices. One of them is Gerald. I don't want him to see me. I decide to leave through the kitchen." Her breath came faster on the tape.

"It's okay, Priscilla," Dr. Devins said.

"They're talking loudly. I'd better hide in case they come in and find me. If they catch me sneaking around, I could kiss my last paycheck goodbye."

A muffled sound on the recording, and then Priscilla spoke again. "There's no place to hide in the kitchen with all these open shelves."

"Tell me what you see."

"Oh, thank God. There's a room-service cart tucked into a corner. It's not supposed to be there, but it has a floor-length skirt. I think I can fit underneath. I'm going to hide there. But the door to the kitchen is opening. Please, don't let them find me."

"Who's in the kitchen with you?"

"Gerald, one of the poker dealers and a woman who works as a service provider."

Priscilla's face drained of color as she listened to her voice on the tape. Luc held out his hand toward her, and she placed her hand in his.

"Service provider?" Dr. Devins's voice remained calm.

"A service provider is another name for high-priced escorts. I think her name is Cassandra."

"What was the dealer's name?"

"I don't know."

"Focus on the conversation. What are they saying?"

Priscilla groaned on the tape. "They're arguing, something about a plan to cheat a high roller."

"Can you see them?"

"Yes, they're standing to the left of the door, so no one walking by could see them from the hallway."

"But you can see them," Dr. Devins said.

"I'm peeking through an opening in the drape." Priscilla's voice hitched on the tape.

"Are they still arguing?"

"No. Someone else is here with them."

"Can you describe the person?"

"A man, about six feet tall. He's wearing jeans and a black turtleneck. He's got dark brown hair, is clean-shaven and has on dark sunglasses, the ones with the mirror reflection."

"Aviator glasses?"

"Yes, like those. Strange, because it's late."

"Do you know what time it is?"

"Around four thirty in the morning." Priscilla cleared her throat. "Gerald's speaking, and he sounds angry."

"What's he saying?"

"He keeps calling the guy 'buddy,' and telling him to leave the kitchen. The man only smiles at Gerald. Not a very nice smile at all. I'm suddenly cold."

"What else do you notice, Priscilla?"

"That the stranger has on black leather gloves. It's much too hot for gloves."

Priscilla gripped Luc's hand tightly as she listened.

"What's happening now?" Dr. Devins asked in the same relaxed tone.

"The dealer just told the man to leave, but the man merely shook his head. He's raising his right hand." She drew in a sharp breath. "He's got a gun!"

She shivered and Luc let go of her hand to put his arm around her shoulders. She burrowed against him as her voice on the tape continued to recount that terrible night.

"Priscilla?" Dr. Devins spoke her name very gently.

"The gun has a long barrel. The man is pointing it at the dealer." Her voice had a surreal quality, as if she couldn't quite believe what she was seeing.

She gasped on the recording. "The man just shot the dealer between the eyes. He collapsed onto the floor." Her voice shook. "There's so much blood."

"Priscilla, what do you see now?"

"It all happens fast. The man aims his gun at Cassandra and shoots. Gerald moves toward the door, but the man shoots him in the back. The man walks up to the bodies, and I hear three more shots in quick succession." She paused. "Why did he kill them?"

She rested her head against Luc's shoulder as the tape continued.

"I must be quiet." Her voice dropped to a whisper. The agents leaned forward.

"He mustn't hear me. Please don't let him hear me."

Luc hugged Priscilla closer to him as if he could help her absorb the memories of what happened that night. If only he'd accompanied her back to the casino, he could have prevented her seeing the murders. But she had insisted on going alone to avoid detection, and thus had been in the wrong place at the wrong time. Now he could only hold her shaking body, and pray that Culvert would be recaptured soon to put an end to this nightmare.

SIXTEEN

Priscilla trembled as she listened to herself describe the shooting. The pressure of Luc's arm around her was the only thing keeping her together. Memories of that night continued to flow through her mind like the spray of water rinsing away shampoo.

"Where's the shooter, Priscilla?" Dr. Devins asked on the recording.

"He's picking up the shell casings," she answered him, her voice thin and reedy, and her panic apparent in her fast delivery. "Now he's dropping them into the pocket of his jeans. He pushes his sunglasses up on the top of his head. I think he's looking to make sure he hasn't missed one."

"I'm so…" Her voice caught in her throat on the tape, as if holding back a sob. "I'm scared that he'll search the kitchen."

Dr. Devins turned off the recording. "That's where we ended the session."

Priscilla fought the urge to move closer to Luc, to draw strength from his presence. She focused on relaxing her shoulders and taking measured breaths to calm her racing pulse.

The older marshal spoke up. "Dr. Devins, in the case

notes, you talked about her leaving the kitchen and calling for help. Can you go over that again? Maybe Priscilla has remembered more details after hearing the recording."

"Marshal, would you mind telling us your names again?" Luc interjected with a wry smile that turned the corners of his mouth up in an endearing manner. Priscilla could get used to seeing smiles like that on a regular basis.

"Too many names to recall in too short a span, eh?" The younger marshal smiled.

"Something like that," Luc conceded.

"I'm Marshal Frank Jarvis." The older man pointed to his colleague. "And this is Marshal Steve Smith."

"Yes, Smith's my real last name—not an alias." Smith winked at them, his easy manner defusing some of the building tension in the room. "When you're ready, Priscilla, please continue."

The humorous introductions gave Priscilla time to regroup from the recording session. Mac had vouched for Smith and Jarvis, and that was enough for her to trust them. She straightened with a slight shrug to dislodge Luc's arm from around her shoulders and reached for her water bottle. While she found comfort in the closeness, it was difficult for her to concentrate when all she wanted was to snuggle deeper into Luc's embrace and forget all about Culvert.

"The hypnosis brought clarity to the event, and I think I've recalled more details." She closed her eyes, allowing the events of that evening to play through her mind like a filmstrip. "Culvert didn't see me. He didn't notice my hiding place on the room-service cart. He left a couple of minutes later, but still I waited. My legs fell asleep, but I ignored the discomfort. I had to be sure he was gone."

She paused, allowing her thoughts to coalesce before continuing. "I could barely stand up when I finally emerged. I spent a moment stamping circulation back into my legs. I kept my eyes away from the bodies on the other side of a counter. I knew they were dead." Her voice broke, and Luc rubbed her back. The motion calmed her rising anxiety.

"What did you do next?" Jarvis asked.

"I probably watched way too many gangster movies, but his actions made me think the shooter was a hit man. That scared me, and I didn't want to risk anyone knowing what I had seen before I talked to the marshals."

Jarvis and Smith exchanged a glance. "Why the marshals and not the local police?"

She swallowed down the bitterness of her past, but forced herself to continue. "My father was a cop, the casino strip his last beat. He was killed responding to an assault in a back alley behind one of the casinos when I was sixteen."

"Oh, Priscilla. I'm sorry." Luc squeezed her shoulders, then returned to rubbing her back.

The rhythmic motion gave her the strength to continue. "Thank you. The killer, a low-life criminal working for one of the casino bosses, had been 'instilling the importance of paying gambling debts' to a patron and hadn't liked the interruption. He only served eleven years because it wasn't a premeditated murder. My dad was simply in the wrong place at the wrong time."

Priscilla shuddered, remembering how awful it had been in the days and weeks after her father's death. Her mother, never a strong woman, turned to the bottle, which exacerbated her mood swings. Without her father there to steady her mother, Priscilla had known it would be only a matter of time before she lost her mom too. But that was a story to share with Luc on another occasion.

She drew in a deep breath. "I called my father's old partner, Abe Evers. Abe's the one who contacted the marshals because of things he had heard about the three who were killed—rumors of their connection to the Russian mob. Abe whisked me away to a safe place. Then he contacted the FBI. After federal agents interviewed me, they called the marshals."

"You left the scene of the crime immediately?" Smith queried.

"Yes. I was scared that the shooter would find me if I stuck around. Abe was the only person I could think of who could help me and keep me safe." Priscilla did her best to recall her thought process on that night, but the endless questions about her actions ignited a slow burn inside her heart. "To be honest, it's hard to remember why I did things. I only know what I did." She uncapped her water bottle and took a sip.

"I didn't mean to imply there was anything wrong in what you did." The sincerity in Jarvis's voice lessened the simmering annoyance over being challenged.

"In that moment, I was more concerned with evading the security cameras on my way out of the casino. I didn't want to be caught on tape anywhere near the kitchen. I feared the shooter might hear about any potential witnesses and hunt the person down."

She fought tears. "Like he is now."

Jarvis's phone buzzed, and he glanced at it. "It's Mac." He hit the accept button. "Mac? You're on speaker with Dr. Devins, Smith, Luc and Priscilla."

"We're at the motel...room... Whitehurst." Mac's voice faded in and out.

"Mac? You're breaking up. You're at the motel where Rachel Whitehurst is staying?" Jarvis leaned in closer to the phone he'd placed on the table.

"Yes." Mac's voice came in crystal clear. "The FBI, along with our guys, are consulting with the local sheriff's department. We've confirmed with the manager that Whitehurst is in room 223 on the upper level of the motel."

"What's the plan?" Smith called from his position slightly behind Dr. Devins.

"The other marshals are starting up the stairs to the room, with the sheriff's men providing backup on the ground to ensure she doesn't slip through our fingers."

"Okay, keep us posted." Jarvis reached for his phone when a loud noise boomed through the speaker. "Mac? Are you there? What's happening?"

Silence.

Priscilla bit back a gasp, panic once again threatening to overwhelm her senses. With a steadying breath, she sent up a prayer. *Please, dear God, let Mac be okay. Don't let someone else die because of me.*

Luc frowned at Priscilla's pale face across from him at the small kitchen table. She kept picking up her spoon, then setting it down without taking a bite of the tomato soup he'd heated for supper. She had adamantly refused to lie down after the news of the motel explosion. Priscilla had paced the room in shock until they finally heard word from Mac thirty minutes later.

News that they had suffered only minor scratches from the bomb's detonation brought color back to Priscilla's face. Mac had said they would all return to the inn as soon as the FBI crime lab finished their initial investigation, but Luc worried this latest explosion might have pushed Priscilla over the edge.

Smith and Jarvis had been in conference in a bedroom with the door ajar. A new set of marshals stood guard outside the suite's door and another pair roamed the inn's perimeter.

Priscilla remained uncommunicative, her thoughts tucked deep inside. All attempts to draw her out had been met with an apologetic "I need some time to think."

"Hey." He reached across and touched her hand. "It will be okay."

"Will it?" She snatched her hand away from his. "I'm not sure how much more of this I can take. Being in witness protection all these years hasn't been too hard. I didn't have any family left, giving me little temptation to contact anyone from my old life. While I'm sure Culvert knows about the witness protection program, there's no indication he knew about me."

"I know it's been a difficult few days." Luc remained seated at the table, torn between wanting to wrap his arms around Priscilla and keeping his distance.

She shoved back her chair and stood. "Do you?"

He opened his mouth to reply, but she didn't give him a chance.

Her eyes flashed. "You know, this all started because you decided now would be a great time to walk back into my life." The tone in her voice shocked him. "Just when did you find me, anyway?"

His heart thudded and his skin prickled. If he answered truthfully, he might sever the bridge they'd started building between them. If he hedged the truth, it would probably make her distrust his motives even more.

"I asked you a question." The hard edge to her voice belied the tremor that shook her body.

His mother had instilled in him that telling the truth might mean temporary pain—like when he'd confessed to breaking her Dresden shepherdess—but it also brought inner peace. "Three months ago."

Her jaw dropped. "Three months ago?"

At his nod, confusion flickered in her eyes. "Then why did you wait so long to approach me?"

Again, he chose the truth. "I was praying."

"Praying?" Her brows furrowed as she parroted the word back to him.

"Yes." He met her eyes, willing her to see his sincerity. "I didn't know why you'd left. I had been searching for you. When I found you, I wasn't sure how to proceed. So I prayed."

"For three months, you've been praying for me." She blinked back tears.

"Yes. I've been praying for you." A knot in his own throat stopped the rest of what he wanted to say for a moment. He swallowed hard, and softly added, "I've been praying about what to do next."

The front door opened, and Mac, Laura, Aldrich and Myers entered the room. Luc bit back a groan at the interruption.

"Mac!" Priscilla hugged the marshal as Smith and Jarvis came into the room. "I'm glad you're okay." She looked at the other three, who wore rumpled suits with dirt streaks and torn fabric.

"Just a few bumps, bruises and scratches." Laura winced slightly as her husband came out of the other bedroom and embraced her.

"And the witness?" Luc inserted the question into the general greetings from the others.

"Whitehurst is dead, whether from the blast or not, we're not sure. The medical examiner will have to sort that out." Mac sank down onto the couch, weariness in every line.

The others grabbed bottled water and milled around the tiny kitchen, finding snacks to eat.

"Do you think she was responsible for getting Culvert out of the hospital?" Priscilla sat down next to Mac.

Luc edged closer, standing beside them to listen to their conversation.

"Culvert is taking care of loose ends." Mac set his lips in a firm line.

"Any sign that Culvert came to the motel?" Priscilla asked.

"Not yet." Mac's phone rang, and he hit the speaker button. "Mac here. You're on speaker."

"Marshal MacIntire. It's been a long time." The man's raspy voice filled the room and the steel behind it caused Luc's stomach to clench.

Everyone crowded closer to Mac, all eyes on the phone sitting on the coffee table.

"Who is this?" Mac propped his elbows on his knees.

What might have passed for a chortle came over the phone's speaker. "I can't believe you would forget such an old friend."

Mac stared at the phone as Laura slipped her cell from her pocket and hit the record button to capture the call. "I haven't forgotten you, Mason Culvert. Calling to gloat over your handiwork?"

Luc put his hand on Priscilla's shoulder. Why was Culvert calling Mac? And how did he get Mac's cell number?

"I've never been one to gloat."

"It's only a matter of time before we find you again." Mac's voice held determination. "How did you get this number?"

Again that laugh, which held no humor. "It wasn't hard."

"Why don't you turn yourself in?" Mac loosely clasped his hands together. If he was trying to project an unruffled demeanor, the tension lines around his mouth betrayed him.

"To you? I don't think so." Culvert's voice sharpened. "I'll take my chances."

"Then why are you calling?"

"I didn't kill Rachel." Culvert sounded aggrieved.

"What?" Mac smirked. "You're calling to report a crime, are you?"

"Just setting the record straight."

"We have you dead to rights." Mac's voice dropped to a growl. "You're cleaning house. You can't stand the fact that we can put you away for a very long time. Better hope a death-penalty state doesn't get to you first."

"I wouldn't hurt Rachel."

"And why should I believe you?" Mac shot back.

"Because I'm not the only one with something to lose."

Click.

SEVENTEEN

Priscilla rotated her shoulders, trying to ease the tension that had converted the muscles into rocks. Forty minutes ago, Myers, Aldrich and Laura had arrived back from the motel, but the marshals sent her and Luc to one of the bedrooms while they debriefed. With the door firmly closed, she couldn't eavesdrop on their conversation, and being kept in the dark added to her jitters.

"I hope this gets wrapped up soon." Luc quirked his lips into a smile. "My sister will kill me if I miss her birthday."

She sank onto the love seat, grateful for the distraction. "Sister, huh? I don't remember anything about your family."

He joined her on the sofa. "My mother's name is Joann, and my father's is James. I'm the youngest of four. I have three older sisters. The eldest is Lucy, who married Paul Bonneville, and they have two adorable little kids. The second oldest is Elise, and she's in South Africa as part of her international humanitarian work. Elise is also recently engaged to a wonderful South African named Zane Okiro."

"And your youngest sister?"

"Octavia is only thirteen months older than me, and

she teaches kindergarten. Not married or 'even close,' as she puts it."

"Where do your parents live?" Removing her sneakers, she tucked her feet up underneath her legs.

"In a tiny little town called Clintwood in southwest Virginia near the Kentucky border." Luc propped his feet on the small coffee table. "My father runs a small hobby farm that sells produce at farmers' markets and area restaurants. He's also been the town mayor for forever."

"What about your mom?" Priscilla tried not to be jealous at the obvious affection Luc had for his family, evidenced by the warmth with which he spoke of them.

"My mother's a surgeon in a regional medical center. She mostly stitches up cuts these days, but she travels all summer throughout Appalachia to the hamlets and towns to offer general medical care to residents who either can't afford to see a doctor or don't have access to one."

"Wow, she sounds amazing." A longing to be part of such a family filled her, and she closed her eyes to fight back tears. She hugged one of the throw pillows to center her thoughts. She couldn't think about the future now, not with Culvert trying to kill her. But until Luc shared about his family, she hadn't realized how much she'd missed having one of her own.

Priscilla sighed. "I wish I knew what they were discussing out there."

"Yeah, me too." Luc held out his hand, and it seemed the most natural thing in the world to slip hers inside his.

"What's Mac's background?" Luc laced his fingers through hers into a loose grip. "You seem really close to him."

"I suppose I am." Priscilla ignored the undercurrent

of what might have been jealousy in Luc's voice, not wanting to discuss his feelings or hers. Instead, she focused on his question. "That's what happens when your life depends on another."

"He doesn't share much personal information."

"I guess that's to be expected in his line of work. He's been my handler for three years, since I was moved to Virginia, but I still know very little about him outside the marshals."

"Where were you before?"

"A small town in the Midwest." She looked at him. "I can't tell you more than that."

Luc squeezed her fingers, and the reassurance that he understood gave her comfort. She hadn't been able to be honest with anyone about her life in many years, so to share even these details with Luc filled her with contentment. "I'm not sure why I was moved. Mac just showed up one day and said it was time to pack my bags."

"You had to change your name again?" Luc's eyes held sympathy. "That must have been hard."

"It was. Sometimes, they let you pick a name, and sometimes, you can keep your first or middle name. I chose to keep my first name, but had to learn a new last name and background details. Since I pretty much kept to myself anyway, it wasn't that hard." Priscilla wouldn't mention the nights she'd cried herself to sleep because of the loneliness. In fact, she'd better shift the subject back to Mac before she started bawling on Luc's shoulder.

Priscilla gazed down at their joined hands. "Anyway, all Mac ever told me was that he joined the marshals a decade ago after a stint in army intelligence."

"One of the other marshals told me Mac was married."

"Yes, although he doesn't wear a wedding ring and

rarely talks about his wife. I asked him about it once, and he said he needed to keep his private life separate from his work with the marshals." She slanted a look at him. "You weren't jealous, were you?"

"Of Mac? Nah."

But despite his words to the contrary, she detected a hint of pink washing across his face.

However, before she could tease him further, Luc let go of her hand to point at the clock on the bedside table. "It's close to six. Want to see if local news has anything on the explosion?"

"Sure." Priscilla relaxed against the back of the sofa, very aware of Luc's shoulders mere inches from her own.

He picked up the TV remote and clicked it on to a local station just beginning its six o'clock news program.

A perky blonde newscaster opened the broadcast. "Good evening. I'm Cassie Nobles. Thank you for choosing Action 8 News. Here's today's top story. An explosion rocked a Motel 6 just outside of Peebles, West Virginia, this morning, killing two and injuring several others."

Two dead? Priscilla hadn't heard about a second victim—just that Rachel Whitehurst had died in the blast.

On TV, footage of firefighters hosing down the smoldering remains of a structure played as the anchorwoman outlined what Priscilla already knew.

"Kent Malloy is on the scene. Kent, any further developments?" Nobles asked as the camera shifted to a live shot, bright lights illuminating the reporter as he did a stand-up with the charred building as a backdrop.

"The Fayette County Fire Department is investigating what caused the explosion. A source speculated to me off camera that the device was likely triggered remotely. As to who set the device or why, those questions have yet to be answered. FBI investigators are on site now, sifting through the debris for clues."

"Have the victims been identified?" Nobles's voice held just the right touch of concern to Priscilla's ears.

"The FBI just released their names. John Evans, the manager, had worked for the motel for twenty years. The other victim, Rachel Whitehurst, rented the room where the bomb exploded. The FBI said Ms. Whitehurst worked at Fairfax Inova Hospital in Virginia. Fayette County Sheriff's Department informed me only moments ago that Ms. Whitehurst was a person of interest in the escape of alleged hit man Mason Culvert, who's been on the run since Monday."

"Kent, did the sheriff's department provide any further details about the Culvert case?" Nobles interjected from the studio.

"Only that US marshals had come to interview Ms. Whitehurst in connection with Culvert's escape from custody following his emergency appendectomy on Sunday."

"Thank you, Kent. We'll be bringing you updates on the explosion in Peebles, West Virginia, as things unfold." Nobles glanced at the papers on the polished table in front of her. "In national news, the president met with…"

Someone knocked on the door, and opened it before Priscilla or Luc could respond. Mac held up two bags of Chinese takeout. "I thought we'd eat in here, as I'm sure you have some questions about what's happening." He crossed the room and placed the bags on the dresser beside the TV. "You saw the news?"

"Yes." Luc got to his feet. "I didn't know they had confirmed Rachel's death."

"I wouldn't have released that information, but it's not our investigation." Mac hauled out several food containers. "We have sweet-and-sour pork, chicken and broccoli, and moo shu beef and cabbage. What would you like?"

Priscilla picked the pork, Luc took the chicken and Mac seemed happy to have the beef-and-cabbage dish all to himself. Mac dished out the fried rice and spring rolls on paper plates he'd brought with him, and handed out napkins and utensils.

"If you'll grab the desk chair, we can use the coffee table for our plates," Luc suggested.

"Good idea. I'll get some bottled water. Be right back." Mac pulled the door to, but it didn't latch, leaving a slight crack.

The marshals' dinner conversation piqued Priscilla's interest as she balanced her plate on her lap.

"The photos of the motel bomb site are very similar to another bombing attributed to Culvert," Aldrich said, talking in the other room. "That other bombing was triggered by a keycard inserted into the door lock. Coincidence? I think not."

The color drained from Priscilla's face. "That poor woman."

Luc put down his plate of food and was about to put his arm around her shaking shoulders when Mac returned with three bottles of water. Mac pushed the door closed with his foot before joining them around the coffee table.

"You heard Aldrich's comment?" Mac passed around the bottled water as both Luc and Priscilla nodded. "We're taking every precaution to keep you safe."

She hunched her shoulders as she toyed with her fork above the steaming pork dish. "I know you are."

But Luc could practically feel the stress crashing off her like waves against rocks. He asked the question that had been bouncing around in his brain for a while. "How can you be sure it's Culvert who's behind the attempts on Priscilla's life and these deaths?"

Mac arched his eyebrows. "Culvert will do anything to avoid paying for his crimes." He speared a piece of beef with a chopstick but didn't pop it in his mouth. "Priscilla's in the witness protection program because she witnessed him shoot three people—at point-blank range. In my professional opinion, yes, I believe Culvert's behind all of it."

Luc swallowed a bite of broccoli. "That's what bothers me."

"It bothers you that an assassin is after Priscilla?" Mac expertly wielded the chopsticks to eat a piece of cabbage.

"No, it bothers me that he's not been successful." Luc mentally slapped himself in the forehead over his poor word choice.

"You want Culvert to succeed in killing me?" Priscilla put down her fork, her eyes wide. "And here I thought you wanted me alive so we could figure out this marriage thing."

Luc shifted his plate from his lap to the table in front of him. "I didn't mean that. I do want you alive." He groaned, frustrated over his bumbled conversation. "Let me start over." He turned to Mac. "How long had Culvert been operating as a hired assassin?"

Mac finished a bite before answering. "As far as we can tell, at least two decades."

"Okay, twenty years. Who hires him?" Luc ignored

the food on his own plate as the idea he'd been thinking about for the last twenty-four hours came into focus.

Mac uncapped a bottle of water and took a drink. "It's been major crime families, both international and domestic. Culvert's the one these crime syndicates call to clean house, like the Vegas shooting Priscilla witnessed. He's also had a hand in the assassinations of minor government officials in some of the more unstable countries."

"In other words, he's so good at his job that people in high places hire him." Luc's stomach growled.

"That's a fair assessment of Culvert's skills. He didn't get caught until recently, and that was because of a two-year-long sting operation in which a deep undercover agent portrayed a potential client." Mac picked up his spring roll and ate it quickly.

"How did Culvert usually kill his victims?" As he asked the questions that had been burning in his mind, Priscilla ate steadily.

"Just where are you going with all these questions?" Mac growled.

Mac's irritation dampened Luc's enthusiasm.

"You said you were here to answer some of our questions." Priscilla ate another piece of sweet-and-sour pork.

"You're right—I did." Mac leaned back in the desk chair. "Culvert's signature shot is a tap to the forehead between the eyes. He always follows up with a second shot to the head as well."

"And the crime scenes?" Luc risked being shut down again, but he had to continue this line of thought.

"Clean as a whistle. Even that bomb Aldrich alluded to just now had been carefully calibrated to do maximum impact inside the room with as little collateral damage as possible."

"I bet Culvert always wears gloves to leave no fingerprints." Luc polished off the remaining water in his bottle.

Mac shoved his paper plate and chopsticks into a plastic bag. "Culvert treads lightly and I mean that in a literal sense. At one crime scene near a lake, he avoided walking in the muddy terrain to avoid leaving footprints."

"Then why has his MO changed?" The answer to this question would be one that could change the direction of the investigation—and keep Priscilla safe.

EIGHTEEN

Priscilla's heart raced as Luc voiced the very question about Culvert changing his MO that had been bothering her since the second hypnosis session. The memory of the cool, very collected hit man didn't jibe with the slipshod attempts on her life. A man who picked up shell casings and walked nonchalantly out of the room where he had shot three people didn't suddenly start acting like an amateur.

"Because he's desperate," Mac said, ticking off the items on his fingers. "He just had major surgery, and doesn't have access to the resources he once did. Three very good reasons for his MO to change." The marshal rose. "Besides, Culvert could be merely throwing us off his scent, making us think it's not him behind the efforts to kill Priscilla."

She scrambled to her feet and put her plate in the plastic trash bag that held the remains of Mac's dinner.

Luc stared down at his barely touched plate of food.

"I know you mean well, but this is out of your league." Mac laid a hand on Luc's shoulder. "Don't muddy the waters with such wild speculation. We all need to focus on catching Culvert. Once we do, we'll be in a much better position to sort out the whys and hows."

Mac took the bag of trash from Priscilla. "I'll take care of the trash. I have to check in with the others anyway. Priscilla, trust me when I say that this will end soon." He left the room, closing the door behind him.

"Do you really think it's Culvert?" Luc's voice had an edge to it she hadn't heard before. Maybe the nearly constant tension was getting to him as well.

"The marshals think so." Her head ached. Priscilla wanted to sink down onto the bed and sleep for a week, but the kind of rest she needed would only happen once Culvert was caught.

Luc got to his feet, his eyes earnest as he took her hand. "Priscilla, you know something's not right with this whole situation. You heard Mac—Culvert doesn't have access to the contacts he once did. How is it that he always seems to be dogging our steps so closely?"

While she drew comfort from Luc's presence in her life during this difficult time, she couldn't completely dismiss that none of this had started happening until Luc appeared at the salon.

Luc relaxed his grip on her hands, maybe sensing it was too much. "I know you think I'm meddling where I don't belong, but it's too much of a coincidence to believe a man as well versed in assassinations as Culvert could miss that many times."

"Mac explained that." Her brain hurt. Too much had happened over the course of a few days for her to make sense of any of it. All she knew for certain was that her life was in danger. Culvert had to be the one behind it all because she'd barely had any acquaintances, let alone enemies, in the past seven years. "Physically, Culvert's not one hundred percent right now—he's still recovering from the operation. It's possible his wound is infected, and he wouldn't think clearly or be able to perform like he's done in the past."

"That still doesn't mesh with all that we know of Culvert. Plus, what about that phone call from Culvert?"

"You heard Mac—he thought Culvert was simply trying to muddy the waters." She withdrew her hands from his. "You don't know Culvert at all."

"You don't either." Luc persisted. "You're making him out to be some kind of supervillain."

Her ire rose to near boiling. She pointed a finger at him. "You didn't see him kill three people as calm as a cucumber." Her voice rose. "You haven't been looking over your shoulder for the past seven years, wondering if the man with the dead eyes was going to ring your doorbell and shoot you in the head. You haven't lived like I have!"

"No, I haven't." Luc crossed his arms. "But you're not hearing me."

Priscilla gritted her teeth as he plowed on.

"Culvert is a professional—these attempts on your life have not been as meticulously planned as missions he's done his entire career."

"You said that already." She shook her head, irritation rising to clash with his obstinacy. "Since you're going over old ground, let me remind you that all of this started when you showed up at the hair salon where I worked."

"I explained that—it's just a coincidence."

"It's that *coincidence* that passes muster, but not the other coincidences that have happened since then?" Anger tightened her shoulders as tension poured into her muscles. "That's very convenient for you, isn't it? How do I know that you aren't behind the entire thing? I've managed to escape being hurt, a few times because of your supposed quick thinking. What if it wasn't quick thinking but preplanned to make me trust you?"

"What are you saying, Priscilla?" His voice turned icy and caused her to shiver. "You think I'm behind the attacks? That I would sanction killing those marshals just to gain your trust?"

"Yes. No. I don't know!" She threw up her hands. "The point is that I don't know you." Moving a tendril of hair from her face, she took a moment to collect her thoughts. "You show up out of the blue, saying you're my long-lost husband of whom I have no memory and boom! Scary *things*, deadly *things* started happening."

"I can't believe you're saying this to me." The pain on his face nearly convinced her of his sincerity. "I searched for you, yes, but not to kill you!"

Priscilla wavered, wanting to believe him. But a life spent not trusting anyone made it difficult for her to put her trust in a man that she could barely remember. Yes, she recalled spending a summer with him on a youth mission trip on the Navajo Nation Reservation, but that was years ago when they were both teenagers. People changed, and not always for the better. What if he coerced her into marriage? What if she had been running away from him when she ran into the kitchen of the Last Chance Hotel and Casino?

"I would never hurt you. Please believe me." Luc reached out for her hand, but she took a step back.

"Those are only words." She choked back sobs, exhaustion and stress robbing her of the ability to keep a tight lid on her emotions. "I don't know if I believe you or not. But if it's not Culvert and it's not you, who could it be? What motive would this mysterious other person have for wanting me dead? Culvert's the only one with a motive."

"I don't know." Luc rubbed a hand over his eyes.

"You don't know." The energy and anger drained from her like water from a bathtub. "I'm going to take a shower, then try to get some sleep."

"Okay." Luc put his hand on the bedroom door, then turned back to her. "If it's not Culvert, then you might be in more danger than any of us realizes."

Luc unwrapped the fast-food breakfast sandwich and bit into it. Cold. He glanced up from the couch where he had slunk to see Priscilla standing in the tiny kitchenette near the microwave. After the frosty way they'd parted last night, he wasn't about to ask her to move to warm up his sandwich.

Last night, while lying in bed unable to fall asleep thanks to Agent Myers's snoring, he went over and over their conversation. He certainly could have been less dogmatic about his idea that it must be someone other than Culvert behind the attacks. In the wee hours of the morning, he had realized Priscilla was right—his actions looked suspicious. He had been hunting her for years. He'd shown up out of the blue, using an assumed name. He hadn't been forthcoming with his identity after the shooting. Yes, he had done all those things but not because he wanted to harm her. He'd started out wanting to find Priscilla to annul their marriage and have a clean slate for any future relationships. Not that he'd planned on finding a girlfriend anytime soon. He had no faith in his ability to sustain a relationship after his college fiancée left him for someone else and then Priscilla abruptly departed after their wedding. Lately, though, he found himself wondering what a future with Priscilla would be like.

"Luc?"

He jerked at the sound of Priscilla's voice, nearly dropping the sandwich.

"May I join you?"

"Of course." He scooted over to allow her more room. The last thing he wanted was for Priscilla to feel crowded by him—even though he ached to be close to her.

Dark circles smudged the pale skin underneath her eyes, attesting to her own restless night. She wore a fresh flannel shirt tucked into a pair of jeans. Both articles of clothing hung a bit loose on her frame.

"About last night." Priscilla set her coffee cup on the low table in front of the couch. "I've been looking over my shoulder, examining everyone's motive who wants to get close to me, for years. It's hard not to be suspicious when that's been my modus operandi for so long."

"I understand." Luc couldn't imagine trying to carve out a life under those circumstances. He admired her for how she'd managed thus far.

She shook her head. "I don't think you do. It's lonely and monotonous and scary all wrapped together. I have very few friends because I can't share anything beyond the surface to avoid accidentally sharing too much. I found it's better to appear aloof than risk putting a friend or myself in danger." She opened her sandwich, but didn't take a bite. "Then you came along."

"And told you we were married." Luc held her gaze, seeing the confusion in her beautiful blue eyes.

"With no memory of you or our marriage at all, it was hard to believe you." Priscilla took a sip of coffee. "I'm glad I remembered meeting you at least—both in Vegas and on that summer mission trip when we were teens. That helped calm my fears somewhat, that you hadn't been lying about everything. Perhaps, when this is over, I can have another session with Dr. Devins and can recall the rest. But the fact is, whether I do or not, I don't see how we can stay married."

Priscilla said the very thing he had been wanting her to say, yet the revelation didn't fill him with relief. He didn't say anything, sensing from her set shoulders that she had more to add.

"I thought about this all night. We hardly know each other. Even when Culvert is caught, there's the trial that could last months. Then there's appeals and sentencing. Culvert has already retained high-priced lawyers. There's no doubt this could drag on for years. I'd have to stay in witness protection until it's over and Culvert's in prison."

Her gaze dropped to the uneaten sandwich on her lap. "I couldn't ask anyone to join me in such a life. Until it's over, I can't commit to anything, or anyone else either." She raised her eyes to his. "I simply won't have the energy to open up, to share all the things married couples should share, because my focus has to be on putting Culvert away for good and staying alive."

The sadness in her eyes tugged at his heart, while the set of her jaw told him she had made up her mind. He wrestled with his own sense of loss at her words. She was right—their parting ways was for the best. But why did it leave him feeling empty inside instead of relieved?

"It's for your own good and safety," she continued. "You were shot in the arm and nearly burned to death because of me. I can't live with that on my conscience."

A part of Luc was thrilled to hear that she had been thinking not of herself but of him in her decision.

But before he could reply, Mac walked up. "Come on—you can finish your breakfast in the car."

"Where are we going?" Priscilla rewrapped her sandwich.

Luc grabbed his coffee and sandwich as well.

"To a new safe house." Mac tapped his phone. "Luc will ride with Myers and Laura, while Priscilla will come with me and Aldrich. Dr. Devins will head out with Jarvis and Smith. We'll take three different routes to the secure location."

Luc didn't like this plan at all. He still didn't believe that Culvert was behind the attacks, and it made him uneasy to have Priscilla out of his sight. "Why are you splitting us up?"

"It's safer for Priscilla. Laura will dress like Priscilla. If Culvert's watching us, he won't know which vehicle to follow." Mac held out a John Deere baseball cap to Priscilla. "Put this on."

Luc had no choice but to comply, but he didn't have to like it. Priscilla tucked her hair up under the cap, and Laura did the same. With identical flannel shirts and jeans, the two women could pass for twins at a distance.

"Everyone ready?" Mac opened the door, conferred briefly with the agents on perimeter duty, then took Priscilla's arm. "Let's move!"

Luc tried to keep Priscilla in his sight, but quickly lost track of her as Myers took Laura's arm and motioned for Luc to follow close behind. In the parking lot, the three groups headed to identical black SUVs. Luc climbed into the back with Laura, while Myers got into the driver's seat. The other groups also loaded into the SUVs without incident.

Laura's cell phone buzzed, and she hit Accept on speakerphone. "Ready to roll."

"Good," Mac said. "Everyone's in place. Stay safe."

"Will do." Laura tapped Myers on the shoulder. "Let's go."

Luc tried to tamp down his unease but couldn't. Something wasn't right. He turned to say so to Laura when a trio of pickup trucks with snowplows attached to their grilles roared into the parking lot. Then the trucks split off, each one accelerating toward an SUV.

"What are those trucks doing?" Laura asked as Myers put the vehicle in gear.

"Oh, no!" Luc couldn't believe what was happening. "They're going to ram us!"

NINETEEN

Priscilla fastened her seat belt. Beside her, Mac conferred via cell phone with Myers and Jarvis, who were driving the other SUVs. She didn't like being separated from Luc, although why that would bother her, she didn't have time to contemplate.

Mac disconnected the call. "Let's go."

Aldrich started the engine. He began to pull away as three mud-covered pickup trucks with snowplows attached to the fronts barreled into the parking lot. "What are they doing?"

Priscilla twisted to see each truck aim for a different SUV. She screamed as one truck slammed into the back of their SUV, pushing it sideways. Aldrich struggled to keep control of the vehicle as the truck continued to push against their bumper, forcing the SUV away from the other two.

Beside her, Mac hit a button on his phone, putting the phone on speaker. "Laura, what's happening?"

Whoomph.

"He's running into us!" Laura barely got the words out before she screamed. Seconds later, an awful crunching sound echoed over the phone.

"Laura? Is everything okay?"

Silence on Laura's end. Their SUV shook as the truck accelerated with more force, throwing Priscilla against her seat belt.

"He just…pushed…our vehicle…into the dumpster." Laura's voice hitched, and then the call dropped.

"The plow's stuck under our back bumper!" Aldrich shouted, his shoulders straining as he fought to keep the wheel steady. "I can't get enough traction on the back wheels to disengage."

Another hit jolted her forward. Their SUV pressed closer to the edge of the parking lot and copse of trees.

She craned her neck to see the third SUV with Dr. Devins, Jarvis and Smith, but another bone-crunching hit whipped her head against the seat back as the SUV bucked closer to the tree line. "He's pushing us into the trees!"

Mac braced his hands against the back of the front seat, his other hand working his phone. "This is US Marshal James MacIntire. We need assistance at the Sleepy Time Residence Inn pronto! Three pickup trucks are ramming our SUVs."

Priscilla closed her eyes as the sound of an engine revving rent the air. *Dear Lord, keep us safe.* Her head hit the window while her seat belt tightened painfully across her lap and shoulders. The truck's impact sent the SUV skittering across the pavement into the trees. The screech of metal crumpling rang off-key in her ears as the vehicle settled against a tree with a sickening crunch.

The air vibrated for a split second before an eerie silence descended as if a tarp had been tossed over the SUV. Priscilla opened her eyes and gasped for breath. The entire right side had folded in on itself. Beside her, the metal frame pressed around Mac's still body.

"Mac?" Her voice came out at barely a whisper. She cleared her throat and tried again. "Mac?"

No response.

"Marshal Aldrich?" From her position behind the driver's seat, she couldn't clearly see the marshal. The airbag had deployed and his body slumped forward slightly. She called his name again, but he didn't move. The only sound she heard was the roar of engines growing fainter—a sound she hoped indicated that the trucks had done their damage, then left.

With shaking hands, she unclipped her seat belt, her body falling forward as the belt released. A quick inspection revealed no broken bones or major lacerations. Her shoulder ached and her head hurt.

Just as she reached for Mac, her door creaked. Someone yanked it open. Her heart leaped with relief. Help had arrived.

"I can't tell how bad they're hurt." She slid gingerly out of the vehicle to allow her rescuer access to the marshals. When her feet hit the uneven ground, she stumbled.

Someone reached out a gloved hand to steady her. For a long moment, she stared at the black leather-encased hand around her elbow. Then she raised her head to look straight into the face of Mason Culvert.

The coldness of his gray eyes galvanized her into action. With a jerk, she freed her arm from his grasp, then pivoted as she stepped closer to him to drive her elbow into his stomach—with any luck, her aim would hit him where he'd had surgery a few days ago. Her movement caught him off guard and he fell back, giving her just enough space to dart to the left.

Dodging around a pair of trees, she ran toward the parking lot, less than twenty-five feet away. Priscilla didn't dare risk a glance back as she burst out of the woods and onto the gravel at the verge of the asphalt. Her heart pounded and her head ached as she tried to figure out which way to run.

One SUV had been shoved against a dumpster at the far right of the lot, while the third SUV had crashed into the stand-alone manager's office. Sirens wailed in the distance. All three pickup trucks had disappeared, leaving behind skid marks, crushed metal and the smell of burnt rubber.

The road's entrance would bring her into contact with the first responders on their way. She took one step. Then Culvert wrapped an arm around her waist, yanking her back against his solid chest. Something hard and cold pressed against her temple.

"Not a sound. If you don't come with me quietly and quickly, I will shoot you, then take out the marshals and your husband as well." The steel behind his voice convinced her that to disobey would mean certain death— for herself and everyone else.

She nodded slowly.

"Good." He placed his hand on her right shoulder, moving the gun to the small of her back. "This way."

Once at the tree line, Culvert pushed her deeper into the woods, following a barely discernible path. Stumbling over tree roots and brambles, she managed to keep herself upright as they progressed deeper into the woods. Culvert didn't say a word, but his fingers dug into her shoulder as he forced her forward.

Priscilla's breath caught. Her head swam as a wave of dizziness crashed over her. Over and over in her mind, she prayed for the safety of Luc and the others, for her own safety, for them to find her and recapture Culvert. A stitch in her side competed with her bruised shoulder for attention, but she could only walk on, propelled by the man she had been running from for seven years.

After what she estimated to be about half an hour, he jerked her to the right onto a more well-beaten path. Less than a minute later, the path ended in a clearing where an old beat-up pickup truck was parked. She squinted at the truck, something familiar about its shape and faded blue color. Then it dawned on her. It was the truck that had nearly run them off the road right after the shooting in the salon. Had that really been only four days ago?

"Get in." Culvert shoved her toward the driver's side.

Priscilla considered running for it, but his hand clamped down on her shoulder again.

"Don't even think about it." He reached around her to open the driver's-side door.

She swallowed hard to keep from screaming in frustration at being in his power. Climbing into the truck was like climbing into her casket. Culvert crowded her over to the passenger side of the bench seat. The passenger's-side door had been wired shut, no inside handle. No escape. Thank goodness the bench seats at least had seat belts, and she scrambled to put hers on while he started the truck. Cool air blasted from the vents and Priscilla leaned forward to adjust the direction of the air as a cover for sneaking a look in the side mirror. Only trees reflected in the mirror.

"Unless you want me to blow off that pretty head of yours, stay still."

She straightened, willing herself to stay calm. "Where are you taking me?"

He chuckled under his breath. "A little place down the road where we won't be disturbed."

Priscilla couldn't suppress a shudder. Her pulse accelerated along with the pain in her head. Why he hadn't killed her in the SUV, she didn't know. But she had no doubt that he would snuff out her life once they reached their destination.

Luc opened his eyes and groaned at the sunlight streaming directly into his vision. The acrid smell of burnt rubber and gasoline hit him at the same time pain radiated from his left shoulder through his upper arm where he'd been shot.

He clenched his jaw and redirected his focus from the pain to taking inventory of his body. Feet, lower legs— all moved without pain. Ditto for his fingers, hands and forearms. He touched his forehead. His hand came away sticky with blood from a cut, but at least the blood wasn't streaming down his face.

The crushed frame of the SUV bracketed him in a cocoon of metal, but with effort, he was able to turn his head to the left. Laura appeared to be in worse shape, as her side of the SUV had been crushed against the dumpster, pushing the metal into the left side of her body.

"Laura?"

No response.

"Myers?"

Silence.

Luc fumbled to release his seat belt. The clip had become shoved down into the seat and it took him several minutes to undo the clasp. The quietness of the scene made his heart skip a beat. Priscilla. In the milieu of coordinated attacks on the SUVs, he'd lost sight of Priscilla's SUV. He had to find her, but he couldn't leave Laura and Myers without checking them first. *Lord, please be with Priscilla, let her be okay. Get her the help she needs.*

He moved closer to Laura and placed his fingertips on

her neck. A faint but steady heartbeat pulsed. Luc tried to assess her injuries, but his first-aid training had been years ago, and in his fuzzy state of mind, he couldn't dredge up what he was supposed to do first. He couldn't see any obvious injuries, but she might have internal bleeding. What did you do for shock? Keep them warm. He shrugged off the hoodie jacket he wore and draped it over her still form.

A siren wailed in the distance.

"Hey, buddy."

Luc glanced over his shoulder, his hands shaking from delayed shock himself.

A bearded man with a shaved head stood beside the vehicle. "I called 911 after seeing what those trucks did to the SUVs. Medical help's on the way. You okay?"

"I think so, but she's unconscious. I can't see the driver clearly. I don't know about him."

"You stay put, and I'll see if I can get to the driver through the front passenger door." The burly man wrestled with the door for a few moments before it gave with a screech that set Luc's teeth on edge. The SUV shifted as the man added his weight to the vehicle.

Lord, please be with Priscilla, Luc prayed again as the man in the front punched down the airbag in front of Myers.

"What's his name?" The Good Samaritan whipped out a bandanna.

"Myers. He's a US marshal." From Luc's position near Laura, Luc could see only the back of Myers and the man beside him.

"Marshal?" the man called, his voice loud and insistent. "Can you hear me?"

Beside him, Laura stirred. Luc directed his attention to her face as her eyes fluttered open. "Laura, it's Luc. Try not to move until we can assess your injuries."

In the front of the vehicle, the man again tried to rouse Myers.

Laura blinked as if trying to focus her vision. "What happened?"

"A pickup truck rammed us into the dumpster." Luc kept his attention focused on Laura. "How's your head?"

Laura grimaced. "Hurts." She moved her arms cautiously.

"What about your limbs? Are your legs okay?" Luc kept his focus on Laura's pale face as she slowly touched her legs.

"I feel like someone walloped me hard, but I don't think anything's broken." Laura's eyelids flickered down, but she managed to open them wide again. "What about Myers?"

"He's unconscious but breathing," the man in the front seat replied. "His pulse appears steady."

The sirens suddenly sounded much louder, and through the shattered back window of the SUV, Luc counted three fire trucks and two ambulances racing into the parking lot, followed by a couple of sheriff cruisers. "Help's here."

Laura groaned. "Is Steven okay? Priscilla?"

"I can't see the other vehicles, but I'll check as soon as someone comes to take care of you." Luc ached to find Priscilla, to see if she was okay. His stomach twisted into knots at not knowing what had happened to her. The attack had been coordinated, which meant that someone, probably Culvert, had a plan beyond disabling the SUVs.

Three firefighters ran up to their vehicle.

The man in the front seat quickly moved out of the way and one of the firefighters took his place beside Myers.

"Sir, are you okay?" a firewoman called from outside the vehicle.

"I think so," Luc said as two other firefighters used a crowbar to open the back passenger-side door.

The firewoman leaned in to assess Luc, reaching for his pulse. "Good and steady."

"I'm fine, but she was unconscious." He pointed to Laura.

The firefighter reached across Luc to take Laura's pulse. Then she turned to speak to the third firefighter. Returning her attention to Luc, she said, "We're going to get a collar around you and get you onto a board."

If he were immobilized, he wouldn't be able to check on Priscilla. "No, I can get out myself."

"Sir, you could be hurt and not know it." The firewoman spoke firmly, her hand on the door frame.

Luc didn't have time for this. Priscilla needed him. "I'm getting out now."

The firefighter shook her head. "Suit yourself."

Luc swung his feet out of the SUV. As soon as his feet hit the ground, his knees wobbled, but he managed to stay upright. The firewoman scrambled into the back seat next to Laura.

The third firefighter helped him sit a few feet away from the SUV. "You sure you don't want a gurney?"

Luc nodded. He offered an olive branch, knowing that the sooner someone gave him the once-over, the sooner Luc could find Priscilla. "You can check me out here."

The firefighter took Luc's wrist between his fingers. "Let me get your pulse."

More ambulances and law-enforcement personnel poured into the parking lot, blocking Luc's view of the other SUVs.

"What's your name?" The firefighter ran his hands down Luc's arms, then legs, to check for broken bones.

"Luc Langsdale." He could see emergency personnel swarming toward the other two vehicles, one of which landed nearly in the trees, the other by the manager's office.

The firefighter pointed to the bulky bandage under Luc's shirtsleeve. "What happened?"

Luc settled for a half-truth instead of saying he'd been shot a few days earlier, which would only invite more questions. "It's just a scratch."

"Hmm." The firefighter eyed him for a moment, then peppered Luc with more questions before strongly recommending Luc go to the hospital for further evaluation. "You sit tight, and we'll get you transported to the hospital soon." He jogged off to find an ambulance for Luc.

Luc pushed himself to his feet, staggered just a little to gain his balance and headed off toward the tree line. He'd check that SUV first for Priscilla. As he approached, he could hear Mac's voice.

"I'm fine!" Mac sounded irritated and in pain.

Luc couldn't see Mac because of an EMT blocking the open back passenger door of the SUV.

"I don't need to go to the hospital." Mac's voice had a tone in it that made Luc's heart drop.

Something wasn't right. This wasn't a man who simply didn't want medical attention. This was a man worried about something else.

Luc stopped near the car, his eyes taking in Mac sitting in the back seat and Aldrich being put on a stretcher from the driver's seat. The back door opposite Mac stood wide open, with no sign of Priscilla.

The world spun, and for a second, Luc thought he might go down, but he drew in a ragged breath to ask the question to which he already knew the answer. "Mac, where's Priscilla?"

The marshal looked at him, his face gray with fatigue and pain. "Gone."

TWENTY

"Priscilla's gone?" Luc didn't try to hide the fear in his voice. His body ached but his heart hurt worse.

"Come closer." Mac turned to the female EMT, who had removed a blood pressure cuff from Mac's arm and was attempting to shine a flashlight into his eyes. "I need a few minutes to speak privately with this man."

"What you need is to be thoroughly checked out," the petite redhead snapped, but Mac pierced her with his gaze and she grunted, then stepped back from the SUV.

Luc eased into her place. "What are we going to do?"

"First, I need to know if you're okay." Mac searched Luc's face as if to assess for himself whether Luc had come through the ramming unscathed.

"Yeah, I think so. Of course, the EMTs want me to go to the hospital, but nothing's broken."

"How about the others?"

Luc relayed what he knew about Laura and Myers. "I don't know about Dr. Devins and the other two marshals."

"You need to be very careful."

"I know—Culvert's behind this. To think that he might have Priscilla is making me sick to my stomach." Luc propped himself against the door frame as a wave of nausea hit. With the entire group hurt, everything pointed to how desperate Culvert was to get his hands on the only witness who could put him away for a very long time.

Mac shifted, a flash of pain crossing his features. "You were right."

"I was?" Luc leaned closer.

"Culvert wasn't behind the previous attacks on Priscilla." A coughing fit incapacitated Mac for several long seconds.

Luc wished he had some water to offer Mac.

Mac breathed in and out slowly. "There is someone inside the marshals who's targeting Priscilla."

His hunch hadn't been far off. But Luc had suspected Mac was the one trying to kill Priscilla. If it wasn't Mac—and Luc couldn't detect anything disingenuous in the man's concern or demeanor—then who wanted to silence Priscilla?

"You thought it was me." Mac's voice held a tinge of humor.

Luc shrugged. "You seemed adamant that it had to be Culvert acting alone, and, well, that just didn't add up for me."

"I couldn't let the others know I suspected someone in the marshals of being a traitor." Mac kept his eyes on Luc's face. "But you were like a dog with a bone—wouldn't let go of that idea."

"You tried to discourage me," Luc filled in.

"I didn't want Priscilla to lose you. She's had enough loss in her life. Time for her to have something good, something positive for the future."

Luc didn't bother to correct the marshal's misunderstanding. He had no future with Priscilla. She couldn't risk a relationship while living in witness protection and he agreed it would be for the best for them to part ways.

Mac touched Luc's arm. "You have to find her before whoever's behind these attempts does."

"If Culvert's not behind the previous attacks, why did he kidnap Priscilla?" Luc could see Mac was tiring. The EMT hovered a few feet away, while law-enforcement personnel milled about the accident scene.

"Leverage? If Priscilla's a danger to this person, then perhaps Culvert wants to trade."

A chill settled around Luc's heart. "You mean Priscilla's life for leaving Culvert alone?"

"Perhaps. I'm not sure about that part."

"And you have no idea who's the one behind all this?"

"I have an idea. It's best if you don't trust anyone except me." Mac thrust his phone into Luc's hands. "Take my phone. On my last trip to headquarters, I had our tech gurus install a new app—one that tracks the location of incoming calls."

Luc didn't get it at first. Then the implication dawned on him. "You have the last known location of Culvert from his latest phone call."

"That's right. He must be near here." Mac began to cough again, and this time a longer bout racked his body.

The EMT approached the vehicle. "Sir, an ambulance is here to transport you to the hospital."

"I need one more minute." Mac's severe tone prompted the redheaded EMT to step back once more.

"You have sixty seconds. Then we're loading you up."

Mac nodded. "I have another cell phone number programmed in there. Let me know when you've found Culvert."

"I will." Luc's heart raced. "But I don't have any

wheels. I doubt Culvert's close enough to walk to his hiding place."

"Try the dark blue Toyota Camry with a West Virginia license plate XWF 1243 at the far end of the parking lot. The keys will be in the wheel well of the front passenger's-side tire." Mac closed his eyes and slid his head back. "I called in a favor from a friend in local law enforcement, and he dropped it off for me this morning. I had a feeling an extra set of wheels might come in handy."

The EMT shouldered her way past Luc, another pair of emergency technicians with a stretcher right behind her. "Sir, we need to get you ready for transport."

Luc stepped back, clutching the phone. "I'll find her, Mac."

The marshal opened his eyes to meet Luc's gaze. "Bring her home safe."

"Sit down and don't move." Culvert shoved Priscilla toward a sagging couch in front of an empty fireplace.

One look at her captor's scowling face had her sinking onto the scratchy brown sofa without a word. As Culvert lit an ancient camping lantern, she glanced around the cabin. From the outside, it had the look of dereliction with its sagging gutters. While outside the morning sun had been shining, the cabin—tucked into a small clearing in an overgrown forest—had boarded-up windows that allowed only slivers of sunlight to filter inside. The shutters hung like drunken sailors after a night on the town, and if the outside had ever been painted, there was no sign of that now.

Inside was only marginally better—at least the ceiling and walls didn't have gaping holes or wood rot. The entire structure had a cold dampness that had penetrated her bones within minutes. But the one room had only a small kerosene heater. She hadn't seen a working kerosene heater in ages, as most people viewed them as dangerous. But she didn't care as long as it warmed her up. The lantern provided enough light to drive the shadows back into the corners.

A crate with dry and canned goods and a sleeping bag and mat in one corner with a stack of books on the floor indicated Culvert must have been using the cabin as base for a few days. Somehow, seeing the books made the man seem more human and less of a monster. She couldn't puzzle out why he hadn't killed her outright. If he was behind all the recent attempts on her life, why hadn't he simply killed her in the SUV or dragged her into the woods to shoot her, then bury her body?

Worry about Luc gnawed at her. *Please, Lord, let him be okay. Let Mac and the other marshals be okay too.*

Culvert moved to the front window, maneuvering one of the boards to peer outside. When he let go of the wood, it swung back in place. He angled a camping chair to have eyes on the front door and couch, then pulled out his smartphone.

Priscilla studied the cold-blooded killer as he sat with his head tilted down, his attention on the phone screen. His appearance mirrored the man she'd seen murder those three people in the kitchen of the Last Chance Hotel in Las Vegas seven years ago. When giving her testimony to an FBI agent in the aftermath of the shooting, she had learned that all three had been involved in numerous criminal activities that included blackmail and skimming from the casino. The victims hadn't been without fault, but that didn't make killing them any less of a crime.

While her body felt only bruised from the crash, she

couldn't seem to shake the coldness. She leaned closer to the heater, rubbing her hands together and staring into the yellow-orange flame. Gradually, as her body temperature rose with the room's, her heart rate settled down to normal.

Fear still nibbled at the edges, but anger at her situation fueled her thoughts. If she was going to die, she wanted some answers. She would simply ask Culvert her most pressing questions. What was the worst he could do to her? She had spent years on the run, and she was tired of running, tired of looking over her shoulder, of watching every word that came out of her mouth, of holding people at arm's length. She wanted her life back—or she didn't want a life at all.

She shot a quick prayer heavenward. *Lord, please help me.*

Taking a deep breath, she took the plunge. "Why didn't you just shoot me?" Her words cracked across the cabin, breaking the silence.

Culvert's head snapped up. He fixed steely gray eyes on hers with an intensity that made her wish she hadn't voiced the question.

When he didn't answer, she swallowed hard but refused to back down. In for a penny, in for a pound, as her grandmother used to say. "Why did you kidnap me instead of killing me?"

"Why would I want to kill you?" Culvert's lips twisted into a menacing smile that turned her insides to jelly.

She blinked several times in rapid succession, then blurted, "But you've been trying to kill me for the past four days."

"Have I?" His enigmatic smile lingered, now infuriating her rather than frightening her.

If he was going to claim innocence—which no one would believe, given his history—then she would enlighten him to all the times she'd nearly been killed this week. "It started Monday at the hair salon, where you tried to shoot me and ended up grazing Luc's upper arm."

"Ah, the missing and found husband." Culvert fiddled with his phone, somersaulting it end over end on his crossed leg. "Go on."

Amusement colored his tone, jacking up her annoyance. "You nearly ran us off the road in that pickup truck parked outside this very cabin." She ticked off the incidents on her fingers. "On Monday night, you set fire to the safe house where we were staying, then knocked me out at the clinic. Followed by shooting at us at the second safe house, with one marshal killed."

She paused. "Which brings us to the explosion at the motel where Rachel was killed."

He stopped rolling the phone, but he didn't say a word. The air seemed chillier in his stillness of the movement.

"Then there was the attack with the three other pickup trucks." Priscilla modulated her voice, not wanting to rattle a saber at a sleeping tiger. "Now here we are and I'm a hostage."

"That's quite a list." His voice had dropped to a lower register. "Do you honestly believe if I wanted you dead you would still be alive?"

She could detect no underlying malice in his question, but something in his tone caused her skin to prickle.

"However, you did see me shoot three people in Vegas, and that is a loose end that warrants tying up."

Even as she had listed all the incidents, part of her had known Culvert couldn't have been the one behind all of them. Luc had tried to tell her, tried to express his doubts that someone other than Culvert wanted her silenced, but she hadn't wanted to believe it. Because to believe it wasn't Culvert meant that she had spent the last seven years not really living her life for no good reason at all.

Still, he could be trying to confuse her with the facts he wanted her to focus on. She pointed out the obvious. "Who else could it be? Grammar is dead. The FBI and the marshals say you killed him to keep him from testifying. And you did escape custody while in the hospital mere weeks before your trial start date. I saw you kill in cold blood. My testimony will—"

Culvert cut her off with an impatient wave of his hand. "Your testimony is not as crucial as the marshals would have you believe."

"What are you talking about?" Priscilla gaped at him, her mind scrambling to process this unexpected statement.

He suddenly rose, and moved to a window on the left side of the door, easing back a board very slowly. He put his finger to his lips. "Shh."

She obeyed. Culvert wasn't a man to trifle with, and she'd already pushed him beyond what was safe.

With the stealth of a panther, he moved to the opposite side of the door, positioning himself to be behind it. As the handle turned with a squeak, she held her breath.

The door pushed open. A blond man appeared, sunlight flooding behind the stranger's frame. Culvert pounced, bringing the man into the room and slamming him face-first against the wall with one arm drawn up behind his back.

Culvert kicked the door shut with a bang. "We meet at last."

Priscilla stifled a scream as Culvert placed his handgun against the back of Luc's head.

TWENTY-ONE

Priscilla leaped to her feet. "Don't hurt him!"

Culvert didn't take his eyes off Luc, whose face remained smashed against the rough wood of the cabin's wall. "Sit down."

She sat, quelled by the command but still itching to help Luc. How had he found her? Even with a gun to the back of his head, his very presence eased some of the strain.

Culvert wedged his foot between Luc's feet to separate his legs, keeping Luc's right arm twisted behind him.

"Are you okay?" Luc struggled despite Culvert's tight hold.

"Yes." *Stay strong.*

"Hands against the wall." The hit man released Luc's arm so he could comply with his instructions.

Luc did exactly as he was told. Culvert slipped the gun into his waistband and frisked his hostage, extracting a cell phone and patting down his back and chest with extra care.

"No wire." Culvert put a hand on his shoulder and jerked him away from the wall.

The rug-rash burn on the side of Luc's cheek where

he'd been pressed along the wall brought tears to Priscilla's eyes. She also spotted a cleaned cut near his hairline that likely happened in the car crash.

Culvert brought the gun to the back of Luc's head as he directed him to the couch where Priscilla sat.

"Sit next to your wife, but I'm keeping an eye on you two. I won't hesitate to shoot her right between those pretty blue eyes." Culvert pointed the gun at Priscilla's face.

Luc collapsed onto the couch and Priscilla threw herself into his arms, embracing the warmth of his body as her heart fluttered at being held by him.

"Okay, reunion's over." Culvert nudged her foot. "Break it up."

Priscilla extracted herself from Luc's embrace but kept tight hold of his hand. She looked up at Culvert. "What's going to happen now?"

Culvert gave what might pass as a smile on another man. "We wait."

"For what?" Luc gingerly touched his face with his free hand, his fingers coming back bloody from the superficial gashes left by the wood.

"You'll see." Culvert returned to his chair by the window. "You two can talk, but remember, I'll shoot first and ask questions later." With that, he turned his attention back to his phone.

Priscilla feasted her eyes on Luc. "Are you really okay?" She let go of his hand to gently touch his injured cheek, then flattened her palm against the other side, holding it there for a few seconds.

"Yes, I'm all right, only a few scratches. Did you get hurt in the crash?" Luc squeezed her hand.

She shook her head. "Just some bruises. Aldrich was

slumped over the steering wheel and Mac had passed out. I don't know how badly they were hurt. Do you?"

"Not sure about Aldrich or Myers, but both were taken to the hospital."

"What about Laura and her husband?"

"Laura seemed okay, but she went to the hospital to get checked out too. I don't know about Jarvis, Smith or Dr. Devins. Their vehicle was too far away for me to see what was going on with them." He paused. "I was more concerned about finding you, once help arrived."

"And Mac?" Priscilla held her breath, hoping against hope her handler had come through the attack unscathed.

"He was alert enough to tell me what happened with you, but he clearly needed medical attention beyond first aid. The last I saw of him, he was being loaded into an ambulance." Luc lowered his voice. "Did Culvert hurt you?"

"No. He's been brusque, but he hasn't hurt me." She kept her voice low as well. "How did you find me?"

"Mac." Luc leaned closer, his eyes intent on her face, his voice barely above a whisper. "He said I was right. Someone inside the marshals set us up."

"What?" She shot a glance at Culvert, still focused on his phone. "Someone in the marshals is trying to kill me? That doesn't make any sense."

Luc frowned. "Mac didn't say this marshal was behind the attempts, only that they were involved somehow in this mess. He thought maybe Culvert kidnapped you as a bargaining chip for his own safety."

Priscilla stared into the heater's flame, letting her mind wander over everything that had happened since Monday. She'd hardly had time to think since it all began. The timing niggled at her. Culvert's trial was still more than two weeks away. If he wasn't behind all of the attempts on her life, and instead, someone in the US Marshals Service was trying to kill her, why had it become crucial to silence her now? The marshal would have had access to—or at least, could have probably found out—her location months or years ago. What had set the ball in motion?

Priscilla hadn't realized she'd spoken the question out loud until Luc responded that he hadn't a clue. She elaborated on her thoughts. "I believe the timing of all this is crucial. We've all been thinking it was the trial date, but if we take that out of the equation, what's left? My life has stayed basically the same."

"Except," Luc began, his countenance glowing as if a light bulb turned on in his brain, "that you were about to undergo hypnotherapy again."

"What difference would that make?" She shifted on the couch, drawing up her knee to angle her body to Luc's. "I'd done hypnotherapy before."

"But what if it wasn't that you'd done it before, but who you were going to do it with."

"Dr. Devins? But I didn't meet Dr. Devins until we arrived at the second safe house." She opened her mouth, then closed it. The feeling of having met Dr. Devins before and the uneasiness she'd felt during their initial session along with the shadowy figure of a man outside the kitchen in the corridor all seemed too fantastical to even consider, and yet…something about the idea clicked.

"That's true, but Mac had already arranged the session with Dr. Devins, right?" Luc jiggled his leg up and down as his mind raced.

"No more talking." Culvert glared at them, then turned his attention back to his phone.

Priscilla leaned closer. "Yes," she whispered. "Is Laura involved too?"

He kept his voice soft. "Mac seemed to think it was someone inside the marshals. I'd say that's very possible."

She winced. "I thought Laura was my friend. This is a nightmare."

"As a marshal working with Mac on the team, she would have had access to where you were, even before we actually met her." Luc gave her hand a squeeze.

"But why? What would make a psychiatrist and a US marshal do these terrible things?" The anguish in Priscilla's voice coupled with the tears now streaming down her cheeks prompted Luc to draw her into his arms. He wasn't able to take away her pain or confusion, but he could offer a shoulder to cry on and a warm hug. For now, that had to be enough.

A short while later, Luc looked up at Culvert, who had padded across the room without a sound. His stealthy actions must have aided him as a hired killer, given his ability to move about even in a place as creaky as this old cabin in silence.

Culvert pointed to Priscilla. "Is she asleep?"

"Yeah." Luc tightened his arm slightly around the dozing Priscilla.

The man grunted as if in reply. "Wake her up."

"Are we going somewhere?" Luc hated to disturb Priscilla—she'd had little rest these last few days.

"No, but I'm hungry and, since you're both here, figured I wouldn't need to cook for myself." Culvert eyed him. "Unless you can cook, you'd better wake up Sleeping Beauty."

As if on cue, Luc's stomach growled, reminding him

how long ago it had been since the aborted breakfast. "I can cook."

Culvert gave a mock bow and swept his arm toward the far corner where a camp stove rested on a wooden table. "Then you'd better get on with it."

Luc slid his arm from around Priscilla, then inched forward to gently ease her sleeping form onto the couch. She stirred but didn't awaken. He wished he'd had a blanket to cover her with.

In a box on the floor beside the table, Luc found several cans of black beans, a can of mixed vegetables and a box of elbow macaroni. Rooting around in the bottom of the box, he came up with a couple of packets of barbecue sauce. *Black bean pasta bowls it is.* Next to the propane camp stove he discovered two pots and a can opener. Not much in the way of a weapon, but good for making a hot lunch.

After opening the cans and pouring the contents into the smaller pot, he hit the first snag. Culvert had returned to his position in the chair, his attention on the front door.

Luc walked over carrying the larger pot. "Where's the water?"

Culvert didn't turn his gaze from the door. "There's a pump out back. Don't do anything foolish."

Luc nodded once and headed out back, wishing he had Mac's cell phone. He had sent the GPS coordinates of the cabin before he'd entered the clearing to the marshal's personal cell phone, and now he prayed Mac hadn't been hurt too badly to pass along the info to local law enforcement or the FBI. The pump handle moved easily, water gushing out and nearly overflowing the pot.

The sun had taken up position high above him, but

the trees still hadn't shed all their leaves, leaving the tiny clearing shrouded in shadows. An animal rustled in the undergrowth. Luc jumped and only just managed to hang on to the pot's handle. Water splashed onto his jeans. A pair of squirrels darted from the right to race across the yard, disappearing into the forest once more. Yet his heart didn't stop hammering.

Luc shivered despite the mild autumn day, an over-whelming desire to be inside the cabin's four walls quickening his steps. Funny how he sensed evil not inside the cabin in the presence of a man who killed others for a living, but outside these walls.

Almost on autopilot, he found the lighter, got the stove going and heated the water and the beans and veggie mixture. After adding the noodles to the boiling water, he spotted a coffeepot and asked permission for another quick trip to the pump for more water. Hot food and a hot drink—that was what was needed to boost his and Priscilla's spirits. He gave little thought to what Culvert would think of the meal, choosing to focus on her well-being. Back inside, he put the coffeepot on the other burner and turned up the flame.

"Luc?"

Luc turned from the stove to see Priscilla sitting up on the couch, her hair tousled. "Yes?"

"What are you doing?" She stretched, then yawned. Then her shoulders tensed as she caught sight of Culvert in his post by the door.

"Putting together some lunch." He turned off one of the stove's burners, then moved the coffee percolator to the other burner. "It's nearly ready, if I can find some plates or bowls."

"Let me help." Priscilla came over. "If it weren't for *him*, this would seem like a normal camping experience."

He leaned closer. "We can do this. It will be okay."

"Food ready yet?" Culvert called, his eyes hard as they met Luc's gaze.

"Almost." Luc stirred the pot's contents as Priscilla rifled through the canned-goods box.

Then she tugged out a paper bag Luc had overlooked from underneath the table. "Aha! Success." She triumphantly held up a bag of insulated coffee cups. "We can use these as bowls."

Luc scrunched up his face. "They're not big enough for much of a serving."

"Better than nothing." She produced spoons from the bag as well. "We can always get seconds."

"And thirds." Luc sighed, trying to keep his voice light and the conversation normal. "But you're right—it's better than eating out of the pots."

Priscilla separated out cups for their meal and coffee, while Luc combined the noodles and the bean mixture into the larger pot. He stuck the wooden spoon back in to use as a serving utensil. "Food's ready." The percolator bubbled but the color remained a light brown. "Coffee will be ready in a few minutes."

Culvert came over and Luc dished up some for him. The older man returned to his post, his eyes constantly roving from the door, to the window, to the couch where Priscilla and Luc sat to eat their meal. All three ate the first few bites in silence.

"Not bad." Priscilla made the first comment. "I doubt I would have done as well, given the limited ingredients. Who taught you to cook?"

"My mom. That's how she unwound after a day spent in surgery." Luc went back for seconds, his hunger ramping up as the meager serving hit his stomach. "She insisted that I learn as well as my sisters. By the time we hit seventh grade, we each had a night to prepare dinner for the family. She made us pick our own recipes too." He chewed another bite, memories of those times wafting through his thoughts.

To keep Priscilla eating, he continued talking about his family. "My sisters and I used to fight over who got to cook the noodle dish for that week, as my mom only allowed one noodle dish, one rice dish, et cetera, per week."

Culvert had already gone back for thirds by the time Priscilla finished her first cupful.

"Want some more?" Luc set down his cup to reach for hers.

"Sure. It was quite tasty." Priscilla smiled as she handed it to him. "The coffee looks darker now."

Luc spooned more food for Priscilla, then turned off the burner before pouring them each a cup. "Did you see any sugar?"

She shook her head. "That's okay. I'm just glad it's hot."

"Me too." Luc shared a companionable glance with Priscilla.

When they were finished, only a few noodles and black beans remained in the bottom of the pot. Luc found a black garbage bag in the corner that held a few cans, and gathered the meal's trash.

Luc picked up the coffeepot. "I think there's enough for a second cup."

"Not for me." Culvert crossed to the mantel, his expression hard and his gray eyes cool.

A knock sounded at the door. Luc put the coffeepot down and edged closer to Priscilla.

Culvert removed his gun from his waistband. "You can offer it to our visitor."

TWENTY-TWO

Priscilla leaned into Luc, needing his strength as she watched the front door slowly open. Culvert laid his gun on the mantel, but kept his hand still on the butt.

Dr. Devins slipped inside, closing the door behind him.

Priscilla gasped. The doctor stood there in a jacket with a slight rip in one sleeve—quite unlike his usual polished appearance.

"Ah, I was wondering when you would join us." Culvert didn't move from his stance in front of the fireplace. "Would you like a cup of coffee?"

"I didn't come here for coffee." Dr. Devins darted his gaze around the room, his eyes bouncing off Priscilla's face without making eye contact. A sheen of sweat covered his forehead despite the chill in the air.

Culvert shrugged. "Suit yourself."

"I'm not alone," Dr. Devins blurted out. "The FBI—"

"Say no more." Culvert smiled, the expression scooting Priscilla closer to Luc. "Let's invite them in."

Dr. Devins hesitated.

Culvert removed his hand from the gun. "Does your wife know you're here?"

"She's still unconscious." Dr. Devins wiped his forehead on the sleeve of his jacket. The psychiatrist took a step toward Culvert. "Your little stunt in the parking lot nearly killed her!"

"That's too bad." Culvert's casual tone seemed at odds with his coiled readiness. "That would have been inconvenient, but not too surprising, given her extracurricular activities of late."

"Inconvenient?" Dr. Devins knotted his fists. "Don't you mean convenient for you?"

Luc squeezed her hand, and Priscilla glanced up at him. He dipped his head toward the back door. He wanted them to make a run for it while the other men were focused on each other. She gave a tiny nod that she understood. They stood close to the table, which was about five feet or so away from the back door. To have a real chance, they would need to inch their way back until they were within striking distance of the door.

Culvert shook his head. "No, her dying would be most inconvenient. If she dies, then who will corroborate my story of a rogue US marshal attempting to kill a witness and pin the blame on me?"

Dr. Devins relaxed his fists. "This has gotten out of hand. It wasn't supposed to be like this."

"You weren't complaining when the money rolled in." Culvert's voice had a sarcastic tone. "You were more than happy to do your part, as long as you got paid."

"It wasn't enough compensation, not for the risk."

Priscilla and Luc took a step backward when Culvert's attention was fixed on Dr. Devins, who had yet to acknowledge their presence in the room.

Culvert barked out a laugh. "Sure it was. It was plenty of money. If you had invested it wisely, you'd have had a nice little nest egg now, enough to retire to the country of your choosing. Instead, your wife gambled it—and more—away in online poker games." Culvert snorted. "What I want to know is why you didn't simply hypnotize your wife to stop her from gambling."

Priscilla froze. Laura had an online addiction to poker? How did she keep it a secret from the US marshals?

"She was making progress. Then you had to get yourself captured." Dr. Devins began to pace. "She heard rumors that you wanted to make a deal with the US Attorney's Office. She couldn't let that happen, but you were being kept in a secured facility."

Luc tugged Priscilla back another step.

Dr. Devins pivoted and pointed a finger at Priscilla. "Mac wanted me to hypnotize you. That's when it all started to fall apart."

"Why would that matter?" Priscilla understood Laura's motivation to keep her gambling and association with Culvert a secret, but what did her memories have to do with Dr. Devins? And then she got it. Why she couldn't remember much of Luc, why she recalled only bits and pieces of the actual shooting, why she felt she'd known Dr. Devins before their first session. "You were there, outside the kitchen that night. You were at the Last Chance Casino."

Dr. Devins thinned his lips.

Priscilla took a step toward them, thoughts of escape out the back door fading as more pieces to the puzzle clicked into place. "You hypnotized me there, at the casino. That's why I can't remember that night. You blocked my memories."

"You were supposed to forget the shooting, not the stuff that happened before that," Dr. Devins snapped. "I was rushed during my hypnosis of you, and that's why it didn't work as planned."

Luc put his arm around her shoulders. "You hypnotized Priscilla?" His voice was tight with emotion. "Why?"

"For the money." Priscilla kept her gaze on the doctor as she answered. "Culvert hired him to be on hand for certain jobs that took place in a more public setting to hypnotize any witnesses into forgetting what they saw."

"To pay off Laura's gambling debts," Luc finished.

"The good doctor had to do something to keep his lovely wife out of trouble," Culvert said. "She had borrowed money from the wrong people one time too many. Our arrangement allowed Devins the opportunity to pay off her debts, which, I must say, kept climbing higher and higher." He turned to the doctor. "You really need to get her help with her gambling addiction."

She locked eyes with Culvert. "Why not just kill the witnesses?"

"I don't kill innocent people." He picked up the gun from the mantel, resting it against his right leg.

"A hit man with a code of honor?" Luc sounded as disbelieving as Priscilla.

Culvert narrowed his eyes. "I don't pretend to be something I'm not. The US Army taught me how to kill, and I found I was good at it—very good at it. When I returned from yet another overseas assignment, I'd had enough of the military and decided to branch out on my own."

"But you're still a killer." Dr. Devins's voice had its old confidence back.

"I've known a day of reckoning would come. One's luck always runs out." Culvert stared hard at the psychiatrist. "That's a lesson you should learn."

"What, you believe there's more to life than this?" Dr. Devins glanced around the cabin. "That there's a final judgment?"

The two men eyed each other like boxers circling in a ring, waiting to see who would blink first. Priscilla sidled beside Luc, reaching down to interlace her fingers through his. Maybe they could get closer to the door while the two former colleagues were distracted by their conversation.

"No, more like the old adage 'If you can't do the time, don't do the crime,'" Culvert mocked. "Why don't you tell Priscilla exactly what you did to her?"

Culvert and Dr. Devins both turned to look at her. Priscilla froze. So much for edging closer to the back door. To distract them from where she and Luc stood, she blurted, "What did you do?"

Dr. Devins blew out a breath. "You were easy. Culvert suspected someone was hiding in the kitchen. I waited for you to emerge, then followed you to the break room. The rest was simple." His gaze hardened. "But you forgot the wrong thing! You remembered enough of the shooting to make it dangerous for both of us."

Priscilla tried to wrap her mind around this new information. "But how can you hypnotize someone against their will? I thought they had to be compliant for it to work."

"That's a common misconception." Dr. Devins straightened, a professorial tone coloring his words. "The truth is that most people can be hypnotized quite easily after witnessing a traumatic event. It's often used to help patients with post-traumatic stress disorder overcome that syndrome."

Anger built as Dr. Devins continued to explain the benefits of hypnotherapy for PTSD. He had tricked her into suppressing memories not of the shooting but of her marriage to Luc, effectively robbing her of seven years of her life.

"In a hypnotic trance, clients are able to reenact the trauma, this time substituting what they wish they had done with what they hadn't been able to do in reality." Dr. Devins continued as if addressing a classroom of undergraduates. "Thus, they are able to finally put the trauma behind them and reintegrate fully into their former lives."

"And what about me and the others you hypnotized?" Priscilla stiffened as anger pulsed through her body. "How are we to move on when you've blocked our memories?"

Dr. Devins raised his eyebrows. "At this point, you don't have to worry about that."

The tension in the room accelerated with Dr. Devins's ominous reply to Priscilla's question. Luc gauged the distance between themselves and the back door. They had inched closer, but how many steps remained, he hadn't a clue. Had he latched the door securely when he'd returned with the coffeepot water? He couldn't remember if Culvert had been watching him upon his re-entry into the cabin—and thus allowed Luc to take the opportunity to make a way of escape possible.

Now, with both men's attention on them, there was no chance of meeting their escape objective. Maybe they should make a break for it after all. Or maybe he should rush Culvert and allow Priscilla to dash for freedom.

"Why agree to hypnotize me again?" Priscilla furrowed her brow as she stared at the psychiatrist. In other circumstances, Luc would have gently rubbed away those lines on her forehead in an effort to reassure her. But he didn't want to draw additional attention to them.

"It wasn't my idea." Dr. Devins's voice took on the

whine of someone not used to having his way thwarted. "Mac insisted. I couldn't say no without arousing his suspicions. I agreed." He glared at Priscilla. "You remembered, all right. You recalled every detail of that night, including meeting me."

Priscilla gaped at him. "I did? But the new memories were only about meeting Luc and the actual shooting, not about running into you."

"That's because I had to rehypnotize you at the end of each session, and even then, it wasn't likely to stick for very long." Dr. Devins wiped his hands on his pant leg. "I've been waiting for you to look at me and remember we'd met back in Vegas."

Luc had heard enough. "You told Laura about Mac's request, and she decided that if Culvert escaped, they could kill Priscilla with no one the wiser. Culvert would get the blame."

"Something like that," Dr. Devins replied.

"This still doesn't explain why you kidnapped me." Priscilla's gaze went to Culvert, who had been silent during much of the exchange.

"Doesn't it?" Culvert slapped the gun lightly against his leg, reminding Luc they were still in grave danger.

"You did escape from the hospital, and you did try to run us off the road in Fairfax," Luc pointed out.

"I overheard my lawyers talking about how one witness was going to be hypnotized ahead of her testimony. I figured it was probably Priscilla, because she was one of the few witnesses Devins hypnotized who had disappeared. I asked some of my contacts to find out who was going to do the session, and when Devins's name came back, I knew I had to be very careful."

Luc shook his head. "There has to be more than Dr. Devins trying to cover up his own misdeeds."

"There is," a woman's voice chimed in from behind him.

Luc whirled around to see Laura Devins, her Glock pointed straight at Culvert's head.

TWENTY-THREE

Luc tugged Priscilla closer to him as Laura stepped farther into the room, circling them as she kept Culvert in her sights. The hit man hadn't moved, his weapon still resting in his right hand against his thigh.

"Darling!" Dr. Devins started toward his wife, but was halted by the fierce look Laura gave him. "You're okay. I was worried."

"Not now, Steven." She brought up her other hand to steady the gun. "Culvert, put your weapon down nice and slow."

Culvert shook his head. "I think I'll hang on to this for a little bit longer."

With Laura's attention fixed on Culvert, and Culvert and Dr. Devins looking at Laura, Luc took the opportunity to move back a step with Priscilla. Out of the corner of his eye, he noticed Laura hadn't completely closed the back door.

Laura shrugged. "It will make things simpler when I shoot you to protect Priscilla."

"How will you explain Luc's and Priscilla's deaths?" Based on Culvert's smooth and unruffled voice, he might have been asking Laura if she wanted cream in her coffee.

Beside him, Priscilla stiffened at Culvert's words. Luc tightened his grip on her hand, trying to offer comfort but not draw attention to themselves. He then managed to move them back another half step.

"Unfortunate casualties caught in the cross fire, or perhaps you shot them before I arrived. They were already dead when I managed to take you out." Laura firmed her stance, her gaze never wavering from Culvert. "Either way, they end up dead."

Dr. Devins gaped at his wife. "You're going to kill them?"

"What did you think would happen here, Steven?" Laura narrowed her eyes, impatience radiating from every taut line of her body. "That you would work your hypno-mumbo-jumbo and we could let them walk away? Don't be a fool."

"I didn't sign up to kill people!" Dr. Devins's voice rose. "I helped people forget a traumatic episode, but I never wanted to hurt anyone."

"You should have thought of that when you started a partnership with a hit man, *darling*," Laura snapped.

Luc's pulse quickened. The atmosphere, which had been tense, now escalated.

"I did it for you." Dr. Devins spread his hands in supplication to his wife, who regarded him coolly, all emotion wiped from her face.

Only a few more steps to put them within reach of the door—and a chance at freedom.

"You didn't tell him, did you?" Culvert's voice cracked across the room.

Priscilla jumped, bumping into Luc, who steadied her as he moved them back another fraction.

"Tell me what?" Dr. Devins glanced from Culvert

to Laura, his brows knitting together. When no one replied, he repeated his question.

"Then I will," Culvert said. "Laura's been gambling again."

The blood drained from Dr. Devins's face, bleaching it a sickly white. For a moment, Luc thought the man might pass out.

"You promised," Dr. Devins whispered.

Luc detected a world of pain behind the psychiatrist's words.

Dr. Devins cleared his throat. "You said you had stopped, that you weren't gambling anymore. I couldn't find any evidence on our computers. I thought you really had turned over a new leaf."

"Maybe I just got smarter." Laura tightened her grip on the gun, still trained at Culvert's chest. "I asked some tech guys at work how to wipe away evidence of websites for good. You never even noticed."

Luc managed to pull Priscilla another step closer to the door while the other two men kept their attention on Laura, who still stood a few feet away from Priscilla and Luc.

"How much?" Dr. Devins's shoulders slumped. "How much did you lose this time?"

Laura shrugged. "Six months ago, I joined a new game, and I was winning. I was up two hundred thousand dollars. Two hundred grand."

Luc could almost write the ending to this sad story by the bewildered tone in Laura's voice. She had been in the black, but instead of quitting while she was ahead, she gambled for even bigger stakes—and lost it all.

"How much?" Dr. Devins demanded.

"A million dollars," Laura said with a defiant gleam in her eyes.

The enormity of the sum distracted Luc from their escape. How could anyone lose a million dollars? And then, all at once, he got it. Someone had known Laura was a US marshal, had enticed her to play in a new game, had strung her along with big wins, then decimated her, drawing her deeper and deeper in debt. Having a US marshal owing that kind of money would give those criminals an inside source to finding the whereabouts of witnesses—valuable information they could then sell to the highest bidder. Which meant Laura had a lot more to lose than he'd thought—and they needed to get out of here fast.

"A million dollars!" Dr. Devins echoed, his own body language telegraphing his disappointment and despair. "Oh, Laura, what did you do?"

"What did I do? I did what had to be done to save us." Laura swiveled to point her gun at Priscilla. "She gave me the perfect cover, but now that cover's been blown."

At those words, the rest of the pieces fell into place for Priscilla. Why Culvert had escaped from marshal custody, why Laura had tried to kill her.

"I'm not the target!" The words burst out of Priscilla's mouth before she could stop them.

All eyes turned to Priscilla, who stayed perfectly still standing next to Luc, drawing strength from his form beside her.

"What do you mean?" Dr. Devins pointed to Culvert. "That man kidnapped you."

"But why?" Priscilla pressed on. "Because Culvert needed a bargaining chip with the marshals." She could see she was right by the widening of Laura's eyes. "If Culvert had me, then the other marshals would have to come rescue both of us."

"Laura was trying to protect *me*," Dr. Devins said. "That's why she made all those clumsy attempts on your life. She wanted to be sure you wouldn't remember me."

Priscilla shook her head. "That's what she wanted you to believe." For a psychiatrist, he sure didn't read his wife well. "But she had another agenda."

"What other agenda could she possibly have?" Dr. Devins's voice wavered.

Priscilla concentrated on breathing as the tension made the very air thick. She put into words the truth she'd pieced together. "To kill Culvert."

Luc nodded. "To pay off her debt."

"Isn't that right, Laura?" Priscilla looked at the other woman, who now had beads of sweat on her forehead. "The deal was Culvert's death in exchange for a clean slate with the people you owed money to?"

"Seemed like a fair trade." Laura shifted her stance, raising her arms to steady her aim at Culvert's head. "After all, he is a murderer—he killed people for a living. His death would be justice."

"Which one of Culvert's former clients wanted him dead?" Luc queried.

"Does it matter?" Laura snapped back. "The only thing I care about is that my gambling IOUs will be paid in full, once I finish the job."

Priscilla took a step toward Laura.

"Don't move." Laura narrowed her eyes as she swung the gun back to Priscilla. "I only made attempts on your life to make everyone think Culvert was after you. That way, when you both ended up dead, everyone would blame Culvert."

"But what about you? You can't possibly think you'll get away with killing all of us!" Priscilla couldn't help pushing Laura more, even with the gun aimed at her chest. All her frustration for being on the run for so long spilled to the surface and made her taunt the other woman. "And what about Grammar? Why'd you kill him?"

"Had to have one dead witness to make it more believable." Laura seemed unperturbed by the fact that she'd just admitted to murder.

"And Rachel?" Priscilla asked. Luc's solid presence sparked courage in her to continue pressing Laura for answers.

"Collateral damage. I wasn't sure how much Culvert had told her. They were *friends*." Laura again aimed her Glock at Culvert, who still stood with his weapon by his side and a slight smile on his lips. "Enough talking." Her index finger caressed the trigger.

Priscilla bit back a scream. They should make a run for it. But before she could tug Luc toward the back door, something inside the fireplace exploded with a loud bang and smoke immediately filled the room.

TWENTY-FOUR

As smoke poured into the room from the fireplace, Luc shoved Priscilla to the ground and dragged her under the table. The crack of a gunshot kept him prone over her. "Stay down!"

She coughed. "It's hard to breathe."

Luc angled his head to see if the way to the back door was clear. More shots whizzed above their hiding place. Shifting slightly, he leaned closer to her ear. "Is that better?"

"A little." Priscilla pushed up against his body as more bullets flew past, spewing chunks of wood as they hit the wooden wall directly in front of them.

"We need to stay put." Luc eased back to allow her more room, while still keeping his body between her and the bullets flying around them.

"No, the heater." Priscilla pointed to the rickety old kerosene heater, blazing merrily away only a few feet from their table.

All at once, he understood her panic. With all the shooting, chances were a bullet would strike the heater and trigger a fiery explosion.

"Okay, we'll make a run for it on the count of three."

Luc rose to a half crouch, wedging his body under the table as Priscilla did the same beside him. "One, two—"

The back door flew open with a bang. A SWAT team flooded the area. "FBI! Drop your weapons!"

The shooting stopped abruptly. Luc and Priscilla raised their hands. An officer grabbed Priscilla's arm and hustled her out of the room, while another shepherded Luc.

Once outside the cabin, Luc coughed, his lungs burning from the smoke he'd inhaled. Officers moved them quickly away from the cabin to a group of agents wearing bulletproof vests, who frisked them for weapons.

A sandy-haired older man wearing an FBI vest pulled Luc aside. "Special Agent Jack Cravens," he said as a second agent walked up. "This is Special Agent Jerry Suno."

Suno eyed Luc up and down. "Are you hurt?"

Luc continued to cough as he shook his head. "I don't think so."

Cravens waved over an EMT. "Let's get you checked out just to make sure."

Luc ignored the agents, craning his neck to find Priscilla. He relaxed when he spotted her across the clearing surrounded by three men in dark suits as well as a paramedic.

"What's your name?" Cravens asked, as Suno whipped out a notebook and pen.

"Luc Langsdale."

An EMT hustled up, his medical bag over one shoulder and a bottle of water in the other hand. "My name's Tom. Let's get you checked out."

"I'm fine. I'm worried about Priscilla." Luc started to walk toward her, but Tom put his hand on his arm.

"She'll be taken care of. We need to make sure you're

okay too." Tom handed him the bottle of water. "Take small sips. Do you want to sit down?"

"I don't know." Luc tried to twist off the cap of the bottle but his hands shook too much. The trees seemed to come closer to him as the sunlight faded behind their leafy branches. Luc was vaguely aware of Tom's hand on his shoulder guiding him to the ground, then forcing his head between his legs.

"Breathe in and out nice and slow." Tom draped a blanket around Luc's shoulders. "Concentrate on breathing."

Gradually, the spinning stopped. Luc raised his head.

"Better?" Tom crouched down beside Luc and uncapped the water bottle. "Here you go. You've been through quite a lot. Why don't you take it easy for a little bit? I told the agents you wouldn't be answering any questions for the moment."

Luc sipped some tepid water, trying to refocus his thoughts. He didn't think he could do anything other than sit there, but the need to know that Priscilla was all right drove him to struggle to his feet. He scanned the area, but couldn't find her.

"Easy there." Tom supported him with a hand under one of Luc's elbows. "You should really stay seated for a bit longer."

Luc took a step forward, searching for a glimpse of her, but all he could see were men and women dressed in either SWAT team uniforms or suits with bulletproof vests overtop. "Where is she?"

Tom frowned. "You said her first name is Priscilla?"

"Priscilla Anderson." To the side, Luc spotted Culvert standing in handcuffs between two FBI agents. Good. At least that man was safely in custody again. Dr. Devins and Laura weren't visible to him either. He hoped both had been cuffed and arrested too.

"I'll radio my supervisor and see if she's been taken to the hospital." Tom spoke into his radio while Luc continued his visual search of the area.

"Good news. She's on her way to the hospital, and you'll see her soon, because you're headed there yourself." Tom smiled as two more emergency technicians arrived with a gurney. "Your ride's here. Let's get you loaded up and into the ambulance."

"Is she okay?" Luc questioned. He was about to protest riding on the stretcher, but his legs went wobbly on him. Tom helped him onto the stretcher.

"I didn't hear of anyone seriously injured." Tom conferred briefly with the two other EMTs. "You'll be able to find out for yourself soon."

As Luc lay back onto the gurney, his entire body sagging with spent adrenaline, he turned to the only thing he could do. *Lord, please keep Priscilla safe.*

Priscilla quickly dressed in a clean pair of jeans and a long-sleeved T-shirt after her shower. At least this marshal hadn't gotten her another flannel shirt. She would never wear flannel again.

She had spent hours being poked and prodded in the ER before being pronounced well enough to be discharged. A female US marshal whom she hadn't met before had brought her yet another change of clothes and had finagled a shower for her in the female employee locker room. Her right knee ached, her left shoulder sported the beginnings of a large bruise from the seat belt and her head hurt. The ibuprofen had taken the edge off her aches and pains, and a good night's sleep would help immensely. But who knew when she would be able to actually close her eyes, given the parade of FBI agents, US marshals and others who clamored for statements and information about the last four days.

At least she'd found out that Luc had arrived at the hospital safe and sound a few hours earlier. She'd wanted to see him with her own eyes, but her request had been ignored. Twisting her damp hair up into a bun, she wrapped an elastic hair tie around it and exited the shower area in her bare feet. Priscilla still couldn't believe that Culvert had been recaptured, that the Devinses were in custody, that her life would return to normal—or at least what had passed for normal before Monday. Even Mac wasn't in as bad shape after the truck attack as she'd feared.

Which meant that she could start thinking about the future. A future she hadn't thought was even possible less than twelve hours ago. Maybe a future with Luc, the thought sending a warmth throughout her body. But she was grasping at straws. Who was she kidding? There was still the Culvert trial to get through, then the trial for the Devinses. Besides, she still couldn't remember marrying Luc or what had prompted her to say yes to a man she'd met only hours earlier, despite their connection as teenagers. Her life wouldn't be truly her own until she could leave witness protection—and, like she had told Luc, she couldn't ask him to forsake his own family to build a new one with her.

In the empty locker room, the US marshal had her phone to her ear, but pointed to a pair of socks and sneakers on a bench.

Priscilla nodded her thanks and slipped on the footwear.

"Ready?" The tall blonde smiled as she pocketed her

phone. "I know you're worn out, but do you think you're up for more questions from the FBI if we feed you first?"

Priscilla couldn't summon the energy to return the woman's smile. "To be honest, all I want to do is sleep for a week."

The marshal studied her. "You haven't had much of that lately, have you?"

"Not really." Priscilla sighed. "I can't guarantee I won't put my head down and pass out, food or no food."

"Change of plans, then." The marshal punched in a number on her smartphone. "Special Agent Wilcombs? It's Marshal Adams. Yes, I'm with Priscilla now. She's not going to make the debriefing." Adams paused. "Yes, I understand, but she needs to rest." Another short pause. "I understand. I'll call you in a few hours with an update."

Adams returned the phone to her pocket. "Okay, let's go find you a bed in a safe location."

"Really?" Priscilla could have hugged the woman.

Adams smiled again. "Yes, really. Now, is there anything else you need before we head out?"

Priscilla could think of only one more thing. "Luc."

Priscilla snuggled down on the queen-sized bed, a throw blanket tucked around her as she lay on top of the comforter. Adams had wrangled her a few hours' reprieve. Priscilla couldn't hunker down for a full night's rest, but grabbing a long catnap would be heaven.

"All settled?" Luc leaned over to smooth a strand of hair from her cheek.

"Yes, much better."

He chuckled, then kissed her cheek. "Sweet dreams."

Priscilla closed her eyes, her body relaxing.

"Priscilla?"

Her eyes blinked open. "What's wrong?"

"Nothing, but it's time to get up." Luc gave her a sweet smile. She would love to see more smiles like that from him.

"Time to get up?" Priscilla frowned. "But I just closed my eyes a second ago."

"You've been out cold for three hours." Luc lightly touched her shoulder. "Adams brought pizza."

At the mention of food, Priscilla's mouth watered. She sniffed the air and caught a whiff of pepperoni. "Oh, I'm starving!"

"I thought that would get you moving." Luc moved to the door. "I'll tell Adams you're awake."

Priscilla sat up and pushed the blanket off. "Let me freshen up and I'll be right out."

Ten minutes later, she walked into the small sitting area of the hotel room. Mac sat on the sofa, his arm in a sling.

"Mac!" She rushed toward him but stopped short of hugging him. "I thought you weren't going to be released from the hospital today."

"I'm bruised and battered, but nothing that some pain pills and a good night's sleep won't cure." Mac grinned. "Besides, I told them how terrible a patient I'd be—they had to let me go."

Adams placed boxes of pizza on the coffee table, then handed out paper plates and napkins. "I think what really happened is that he put up such a fuss about checking on Priscilla in person that they let him go to give the other patients peace and quiet."

Priscilla gingerly touched Mac's shoulder. "Are you really okay?"

"I will be, now that you're safe." Mac held out his plate as Adams began dishing out the slices.

Suddenly ravenous, Priscilla sat down beside Mac and bit into a slice.

The four of them ate silently for a few minutes. Luc wiped sauce from his mouth. "What's going on with Culvert and the Devinses?"

"Culvert is singing like a canary, giving details about Dr. and Marshal Devins's involvement with criminals." Adams reached for another slice of pepperoni. "He's not the only one talking a mile a minute. Both of the Devinses have confessed to their parts as well, with Dr. Devins pointing the finger at his wife and Laura Devins pointing it right back at him, especially related to everything that happened to Priscilla."

"With their confessions, will there be a trial?" Priscilla set down her empty plate, her appetite sated.

"Don't quote me on this, but I don't think so," Mac said. "With all the information Culvert is divulging, his lawyer is angling for a plea bargain. He'll still do time—a nice long stretch—but he's negotiating for life in a federal prison if he fully cooperates with the federal prosecutors."

"Did Laura really murder Grammar and stage the explosion at the motel after killing Rachel?" Priscilla asked, her heart aching at all the needless deaths.

"The FBI found traces of the explosives used to make the motel bomb in Laura's trunk, but she clammed up about the bombing itself. Rachel Whitehurst's death appears to have been from a heart attack—we may never know if she died from natural causes or related to the bomb. Her medical records indicated she had a weak heart, but the medical examiner is running more tests to see if anything helped her to have a heart attack before the bomb went off." Mac sighed. "The Devinses have lawyered up, but with their initial confessions, it's likely their attorneys will seek a plea bargain as well."

"What happens next?" Luc took a swig from his water bottle.

"We'll find Priscilla another safe house while we sort through the paperwork and the federal prosecutors work out the deals." Mac patted her hand. "But that shouldn't take too long."

Tears sprang to Priscilla's eyes. "It's really over? I'll soon have my life back?"

"Yes." Mac smiled at her. "You'll soon be able to live wherever you want to." He glanced at Luc. "And with whomever you want to."

Priscilla could hardly believe that after seven years of running, she could finally put down roots and think about the future, a prospect made even more appealing since meeting Luc. But would he want to be part of her life after all that had happened?

TWENTY-FIVE

Two weeks later...

Standing before the full-length mirror in her bedroom, Priscilla swept her hair up into a loose topknot, securing it with a clip and allowing several tendrils to dangle around her face. She hummed along to a Christmas song on her phone's playlist, as she smoothed a few wrinkles from her new red dress. A dab of lipstick and silver dangling earrings completed her outfit.

A knock on her apartment door startled her. Luc was early. When he'd asked to take her to dinner, she had been thrilled—and nervous. Now that they weren't running for their lives, they would finally have time to discuss their impetuous wedding. Given his stated reason for finding her was to annul their marriage, she was trying not to read too much into his request.

She hurried to the door. But instead of Luc, Mac stood on her doorstep, a portfolio in one hand.

"Hi, Priscilla." His eyes widened at her attire. Then his face relaxed. "You must have a date."

"Yes. Luc will be here in ten minutes." Her cheeks warmed as she stepped back to let him in. "I've hardly seen him these past couple of weeks, as he's been working long hours to catch up at work, and I've had so many FBI interviews and paperwork."

He held up the portfolio. "I'm afraid I have a few more papers for you to sign for your exit from the witness protection program."

"What more is there to do?" She didn't mean to sound testy, but she was more than ready to get her life back—and hopefully spend a lot of time with Luc. Maybe she'd go back to school to finish her degree or open her own beauty salon. At least she had some money in the bank after living frugally while inside WITSEC. So many possibilities, but she wasn't going to rush.

"You know how the government needs every *i* dotted and *t* crossed…in triplicate. Don't worry—it won't take long."

"I hope not, as I have a lot to talk about with Luc." Including what he might like for Christmas, now just over a week away. She led him into the eat-in kitchen, where there was space to spread the papers on the bare counter.

"Just sign where I put the sticky arrows, and I'll be out of here before Luc shows up." Mac winked at her. "I heard you had a session with another hypnotherapist."

"I've met twice with a female psychiatrist who's trained in hypnotherapy." She set the papers down on the counter.

"Did it help?"

"Yes," Priscilla said. "I finally remember my entire time with Luc that night in Vegas." What a relief that had been, to have all her memories of that night fully restored to her.

"And marrying him?" Mac leaned against the counter.

"That too." She picked up the pen Mac had laid on top of the papers. "What exactly am I signing?"

But Mac ignored her question. "What are you going to do now that you've remembered everything?"

"I'm not sure. That's what we're going to talk about tonight."

He leveled a look at her, his eyes serious. "I might have had a few doubts about Luc when I first met him, but his actions proved that he's a man worthy of your love."

She couldn't deny the way her heart vibrated like an electric razor every time she spoke to Luc. Today she'd awakened early in anticipation of his arrival late this afternoon, and had spent half the day mooning over his absence.

Mac gently took her hand in his. "Listen, Priscilla. I know you've been through a lot these past few weeks, and the idea that you can live your life without fear is still new to you. But I will say as a married man of eight years who's still madly in love with my wife—I think you and Luc are very well suited for each other."

He gave her hand a gentle squeeze, then released his grip. "Now, let's go over these papers, so I can leave before he arrives."

Mac's words about Luc lingered in the back of her mind as Mac explained the documents and she signed the papers. For the first time in forever, Priscilla believed she could view the future not with fear or trepidation, but with hope, joy…and love.

Standing in front of Priscilla's apartment door, Luc stepped to the left and took one final glance at his reflection in the front room window. He smoothed back his freshly cut hair, then adjusted his grip on the bouquet of red and white roses. He was acting like a schoolboy on his first date, his nerves tingling with anticipation.

During the weeks since the recapture of Culvert, Luc had had a lot of time to contemplate his future, and he'd quickly come to the conclusion that it would be very bleak without Priscilla in his life. Now all he had to do was convince her that their hasty marriage was a firm enough foundation upon which they could build a life together. He'd even taken the bold step of telling his family about his wife, and his mother had immediately insisted Luc bring Priscilla home with him to celebrate Christmas.

Knocking, he waited for her to open the door.

But instead of Priscilla greeting him with a smile, Mac stood there. "Hey, Luc. Come on in. Priscilla will be out in a minute."

Luc entered, clutching the flowers like a shield. "I didn't know you'd be here."

"I just popped by with some final paperwork for Priscilla to sign to complete her exit from the witness protection program."

"I see." Luc was about to comment on how at ease the marshal appeared to be in Priscilla's apartment, when Priscilla walked into the room wearing a red dress that clung to all the right places and captured his thoughts.

Luc sidestepped Mac to cross the room quickly to her, holding out the flowers. "You look lovely. Gorgeous. Beautiful." He stopped himself before he could add more accolades, not wanting to overwhelm her with his enthusiasm.

"You brought me flowers."

"Uh. Yes." Heat crept up the back of his neck as he handed the bouquet to her.

"Thank you—for the flowers and compliments." She accepted the flowers, then surprised him by kissing his cheek. "I'll just put these in a vase. Then we can go."

"You're welcome." With effort, Luc resisted the urge to adjust his tie for the millionth time. He started to follow Priscilla into the kitchen when Mac laid a hand on his shoulder.

"I've already told Priscilla this, but I want to tell you too." Mac extended his hand. "I wish you both the best."

"Thanks. That means more than you can know." Luc shook Mac's hand.

"It won't be easy for her to readjust to life outside witness protection. Be patient."

"I'll try, but I admit that I'm anxious to put that behind us." Luc bounced slightly on his toes, unable to control his excitement—not only over the evening, but the prospect of spending the rest of his life with the woman he loved. He paused, startled by the thought. Yes, loved. Somehow, over the course of those few days together running from a killer, he'd fallen in love with Priscilla.

Mac chuckled. "I can see you are." The marshal tucked a leather portfolio under his arm as Priscilla came back into the room carrying a vase with Luc's roses.

She set the floral arrangement on a small end table and turned to Luc. "Ready?"

"If you are." Luc couldn't keep his gaze off her as she said goodbye to Mac.

"Thanks, Mac, for everything." Tears glistened in her eyes.

"You're welcome." Mac headed to the door, then paused to look at Luc. "Take care of her."

Luc nodded. "I will."

After Mac left, Luc joined her by the door and took her hand in his. "You okay?"

She sniffled. "Yeah. I just can't believe it's really

over, and that I finally have my life back." She squeezed his hand. "I don't know how to live without looking over my shoulder."

Luc tugged her closer, his free hand fingering a ringlet of hair near her cheek. "You have me to help you."

A smile crossed her face. "Yes, I do."

"And we have all the time in the world to create new memories together." He held his breath, hoping she would agree with him.

Priscilla gazed up at him. "I haven't had a chance to tell you about Dr. Hastings."

Concern etched lines in his forehead. "I thought you weren't seriously hurt at the cabin."

"I wasn't." She paused. "Dr. Hastings is a hypnotherapist."

Luc nearly forgot to breathe as he stammered, "Does that mean you— I mean, do you remember me?"

"She was able to help me unlock all my memories of that night, not just the bits and pieces that had shaken loose over the years." She smoothed the lapel of his jacket. "I now know the full story of how you rescued me from my attacker and how sweet you were after Gerald fired me."

"Thank God." He brushed a stray tear from her cheek. "But I'm sorry that means you've remembered more about the shooting."

More tears filled Priscilla's eyes, but she blinked them away. "That part's horrible," she whispered, then gave a shaky laugh. "But the memories of you are much nicer."

That startled a laugh from him as well. "I'm glad." He drew her hands together in his. Now seemed like the ideal time to tell her what he was thinking about their future. "We might have decided to get married on a whim—"

"It did sound like a good solution to my jobless— and soon-to-be homeless—state, since I knew Gerald would blacklist me from casino work," she interjected. "You were horrified at my having no family or close friends to help me."

"I've never been that impulsive in my life, but somehow, it seemed like the right thing to do, especially considering that we had known each other for a time as teens." He gazed down at her, marveling at her beauty that showed from the inside out. The caring heart he'd seen in her on the mission trip had shown through in her concern for his safety as they ran from a killer.

"My own knight in shining armor." She added, "But what I really can't believe is that we chose jumpsuit Elvis to perform the ceremony."

He shared a grin with her, then steered the conversation back to the present. "While I was angry and hurt when you disappeared, I'm grateful that God brought us back together."

"Me too." She sighed and laid her head on his shoulder. "You were the answer to a prayer I didn't know I had been praying for years."

He stroked her back. "Does this mean you're willing to stay married to me if we take things nice and slow?"

She snuggled deeper into his embrace. "Yes." Then she whispered against his chest. "But is it too soon to tell you that I love you? Or maybe I should wait to say it on Christmas?"

His heart swelled with his own love for this woman as he drew back to gaze down at her. "That sounds like a lovely gift, but I was always rather impatient when it came to waiting for Christmas morning to open presents."

"Then I won't make you wait." Priscilla touched his cheek. "I love you."

"I love you too."

"I think we can proceed with our evening's plans, Mr. Langsdale." A mischievous glow lit her face. "Although, since we are married, we don't have to wait until the end of the evening for a kiss, do we?"

"That, Mrs. Langsdale, is an excellent idea." Luc lowered his head as Priscilla stretched up to meet his lips. As the kiss deepened, all thoughts of the past faded away. For now, this moment, holding and kissing his wife, was all that mattered.

* * * * *

Dear Reader,

I'm often asked where I get my story ideas. Most of the time, the answer is simply, "It came to me one day out of the blue." Not so with *Dangerous Christmas Memories*. The genesis of this story came from a news article about a celebrity who didn't realize his Las Vegas marriage was actually legal until years after the fact. Sometimes, truth is stranger than fiction. I knew I had to tell a story about a man and woman who meet and marry quickly in Vegas, then end up separated without dissolving the marriage. But turning that idea into a workable manuscript took numerous starts and rewrites before the story finally came together in *Dangerous Christmas Memories*. And I'm glad I could give Priscilla and Luc's story a much happier ending than the celebrity who inspired the book.

Sarah Hamaker